The Era
Of
My Youthful
Ways

The Era
Of
My Youthful
Ways

Lori V. Lincoln

Croness Publishing
Washington, D.C.

Published by Croness Publishing
Copyright © 2000 by Lori V. Lincoln

Lady Marmalade
Words and Music by Bob Crewe and Kenny Nolan
© 1974 (Renewed 2002) JOBETE MUSIC CO., INC., STONE DIAMOND MUSIC CORP., TANNY BOY MUSIC CO. AND KENNY NOLAN PUBLISHING
All Rights Controlled and Administered by EMI APRIL MUSIC INC. and EMI BLACKWOOD MUSIC INC.
All Rights Reserved   International Copyright Secured   Used by Permission

Never Knew Love Like This
Words and Music by James Samuel Harris III and Terry Lewis
© 1987 EMI APRIL MUSIC INC., FLYTE TYME TUNES INC. and AVANT GARDE MUSIC PUBLISHING
All Rights for FLYTE TYME TUNES INC. Controlled and Administered by EMI APRIL MUSIC INC.
All Rights Reserved   International Copyright Secured   Used by Permission

Grateful acknowledgment is made for use of the following:

"Misty" by Johnny Burke and Erroll Garner

"Congratulations" by Tena R. Clark, Gary Wayne Prim and Mary Vesta Williams

"His Eye Is On The Sparrow" by Mrs. C.D. Martin and Charles Hutchison Gabriel Sr.

"Take My Hand, Precious Lord" by Thomas A. Dorsey

"The Alma Mater (Howard University)"—Words by J. H. Brooks

Library of Congress Control Number: 2001012345
ISBN 0-9710211-1-2

Cover Design: Lori V. Lincoln
Author Photograph: James E. Lincoln
First Printed Edition 2005

Printed in the United States by Morris Publishing - Kearney, NE

ACKNOWLEDGMENTS

"Don't get it right, get it written."

I think of the many times I was stuck or procrastinating because I was being overly critical of this project, and I know how lucky I am to have a friend like Alton Henley to lay that mantra on me. I am indebted to him; to my sister, Ruby, who propelled my first efforts to go to print and to get online; to Marnee Barlow Meyer, who proofed the first, unfinished, really rough draft of the manuscript; and to my brother, Al, whose computer formatting skills saved the day.

Well, I finally got the book written. Thank you to the readers who helped me to get it right: Eryca Dawson, Tracy Holden, LuDrean Peterson, Brenda Henley, Stacia Smith, Kelly Adams, Stephanie Gaines-Bryant, Angela Noel-Peasant, Cheryl Crozier, Nicol Wheeler, Paul Robinson, E. Ethelbert Miller, Patricia Elam, Pamela Lloyd, Trish West—for the technical medical information, Sadia Aden—for the information about Somalia, Rukaiyah Ankrum, Johnson Brown, and even Sharon Barkley, who said she would prefer it if the story were only three pages long!

Poet and author Brandi Forte led me to Elvis Lewis, who has the distinction of having put a copy of my first novel in my hands—a moment I'll never forget! Angela Rogers of ADA Unity Publishers stood by me though the tough part of believing in myself, and in the merit and marketability of this book.

I borrowed a lot of people's names, spirits, personalities, and/or quirks to tell this story. Thanks for being you and who you are to me: Lauren Lincoln, Wilbur Crozier Jr., Louise Crozier, Wilbur Crozier III, Erika Faulk, Louis Crozier, Nettie Culpepper, Rubye and LeRoi Emerson, Billie Jean Jackson, Danielle Harris, Brandon Hamilton, Doris Belle, Kevin McDonald, Jeffrey French, Samuel Walker, Christina Johnson, Kia O. Wyatt, Taira Woodroffe, the late Hattie W. Young, Helene Fisher, Marilyn Fisher, Charon Samuels Ware, Karen-Ann James Miller, Paulette Parker, Joy Clore, Alonza Robertson,

Dr. Charla Smith, Darrian Frazier, Corey Bell, Shaun Samuels, Shameka Hutcherson, Dr. William Jalani Cobb, Andre Burt, Noelle Boler, Kevin Reese, Carlton Ward, Diana Carter, April Clinkscales, DaRell Jones, Elizabeth Lloyd, Cynthia Johnson, Frank Foley, Alfred Alston, Michael Mullen, Sue and Johnny and August Vasaio, Jehu T. Barnes, Lynn McGuire, the late C. Michael Terry, the Larry Chatters family, Dr. Marion Phillips, Dr. Dennis Gaskins, Dr. Angela K. Wamer, DeShaun Watts, Dennis Bell, Terry Austin, Clara V. Burnette, Christina Price, the late LaVant Posey, Princess Posey-Uzzelle, Stephanie Terry, Henry Dobbins, Leander Coles, Mark Ricks, "Renee-Robin-Michelle-Yvette," my friends and family in Gary, Indiana, from Howard University, UDC, North Carolina Health Careers Access Program SEP '89, and all the recording artists whose music marked a poignant time in the life of one young woman.

To Traycee and Julian Gales, Kenya and Amiri Stewart—my sisters and sons—and the rest of you yet unknown to me…one word: catharsis.

—LVL
May 2005

For Alton, my number one fan

In loving memory of:
Njisane Eusi Omawale
Kelly Eugene Mackey
Thomas Lorenzo Cook, Jr.

The Era
Of
My Youthful
Ways

CHAPTER 1

I have a problem with women, but I've loved men all my life. My first crush was on this guy I saw at my father's wedding reception when I was three.

"Who is that handsome man in the white suit?"
"That's your father."
"He's coming home with *me?!*"
"No, he's going home with *her*."

That exchange illustrates just why women are messed up in the head about men. See, **at an early age I was forced to accept that I could not even have the one man who was** *supposed* **to belong to me.** That is where feelings of inadequacy and insecurity begin, and I've found that it's no different for women whose fathers lived with them, but were distant in other ways.

Little girls should have their fathers with them. Little girls need their daddies to pick them up and make them feel small but protected; show and tell them they love them; hug and kiss them; walk around naked for educational purposes; spank their behinds; play too rough; respect them; tell them they're smart, pretty, special and cool; take them on dates; celebrate their victories; console their disappointments; advise and encourage them; spoil them a little; break their hearts just a little; interrogate boyfriends; provide for, protect, respect and romance her mother; and love and respect his own. Unless she has these valuable experiences safely with her own "man," a girl will grow up looking for daddy's kind of love *everywhere*.

Like I did.

I had my first serious boyfriend when I was three years old, in nursery school. His name was Jeffrey—Jeffrey French. He was cute and had light skin and curly hair, just like my dad. Jeffrey only spent afternoons at the nursery school when his half-day Kindergarten let out. I used to call him in the evenings after we got home, and I still remember his phone number: 944-2781.

The next year, Jeffrey didn't come to day care anymore, so my boyfriend was Samuel Walker. I liked his quiet manner, smooth chocolate skin and slanted, almond-shaped eyes. We rode the bus to nursery school together, and we'd sit in the back and kiss—that is, until "Bad, Bad Leroy Brown" came on the radio. Then everybody would stop talking or watching us and sing! because that was our favorite song and the bus driver's name was Leroy! Our little affair ended shortly after Sammy's mommy started teaching at the school.

When this rugged little boy named James threatened to beat me up if I didn't let him touch my panties, I decided I liked him! But no, he didn't get to touch my panties. I thought it might tickle.

Then I discovered (my oldest brother) Bill's best friend, Kevin McDonald. He was another light-skinned, curly-haired "daddy" replica, eight years older than I was...and my brother said he would *kill* somebody. Even so, I decided I would love Kevin McDonald for *ever* and always. Well, he's *still* eight years older than me, and Bill still scrunches up his face when I mention him, but ever and always haven't gotten here yet!

In Kindergarten, Tommy was the cute, curly little boy in my class. He was tall and already had a deep, scruffy voice, but he was stinky! Every day! I sat next to him and held his hand, but I always kept my face turned the other way.

"Look at me," he said once, and I ignored him.

"*Look at me.*" Tommy put his stinky little hand on my chin, and as I filled my lungs with fresh air, he turned my face around toward his. I smiled at him for as long as I could hold my breath, then pretended to need to scratch my ankle. Whewww! Talk about "waiting to exhale!" That's what I thought Terry McMillan's book was about—women who couldn't wait to get away from some stinkin' men!

I've made my point—well, points: 1) that I have always loved men, 2) that I will always love men, 3) that I have always wanted a man who would love me as well as my daddy would have, had he been there, and 4) that it's amazing how soon, in the absence of real fathers, little girls learn to put up with unacceptable s-h-i-t. By the time I was five, I had already dealt with abandonment, a mama's boy, domestic violence, the "Little Sister Syndrome," and B.O.

But I still say all that was better than the deal I got from who?

Other little girls!

CHAPTER 2

Somebody once wrote or said that you could take a brand new baby girl, lock her up in a box away from the world, let her out when she was eighteen and she would *still* be just as trifling, sneaky, catty and conniving as the rest of them. You can't tell me that ain't the truth!

My trouble with girls started in the first grade, when I was six. I was quite popular with my peers, a feat worth mentioning as I was also the teacher's pet. They were supposed to hate and ostracize me, but rather, all the little girls in my class at Douglass Elementary School would follow me out to the playground at recess and spend their time doing whatever I wanted to do. I thought they were my friends, but all it took was a new girl joining our class and they were gone!, turning on me with an uncalled-for *vengeance* before it was all over.

On her very first day, they decided to follow the new girl, Danielle. Being new, naturally she wanted to chase the cutest boy in the class (and the other teacher's pet), Brandon, around the playground. That was fine and everything, until he ran straight for a mud puddle, tripped, fell, and then just crawled right on through...in his white overalls!

That's it. That's ALL THERE WAS TO IT, but here's what happened:

Teacher:	Who chased Brandon through the mud?
Girls:	Lyyyyyyyynn!
Teacher:	And who beat up Danielle?
Girls:	Lyyyyyyyynn!

Later that evening...
Mom: Your teacher called me today. What's this I hear about "Lynn's Gang?" *(as she picked out a belt)*

The next day at recess...
Girls: Lyyy-yyynn…what we gon' do today?
Me: Nothing. Why don't you go somewhere?

From then on, guess who was always off in a corner with her nose in a book during recess? I became a great reader, a scholar, an introvert, a tomboy, …a girl without girlfriends.

I managed to skirt all of their little cliques and clubs throughout elementary, junior high, and high school, but I could never quite escape that girl thing…
First, I started *looking* like one. One minute, you'd have thought I was a boy if you saw me from behind with my baseball cap on, and then the next minute I was all bumpy and squiggly-shaped from every angle! One summer day when I was eleven, I pulled on my jeans and they were a little tight. *Oh well.* I threw on a T-shirt and was headed out the front door with my football tucked under one arm.
"Where do you think you're going?" my mother asked.
"Out to play football."
"Oh, no. You don't need to play with those boys like that anymore. You're a *young lady* now, darlin'. Look at you—you've got little hips!"
So *that's* what had happened. Overnight, I swear!
The guys would surely notice. Getting teased about the training bra had been one thing, but these new hips would be quite another! Agreeing with mom and suddenly feeling a little self-conscious, I opened the screen door and tossed the football to the boys waiting for me in the street.

"I got something to do! I'll catch y'all later!" After a week of not being able to get me outside, the guys had no trouble deciding that they would be just fine without me, especially when they inherited all of my sporting equipment.

Then I started *feeling* like a girl. I wanted to wear cute clothes and makeup, get my nails done, experiment with my hair, and date. Years later, I matriculated at a college where the ratio of women to men was an unfortunate 7:1, making for competition of the fiercest kind, let me tell you!

My (other but younger) big brother, Luke, was taking some extra time to earn his degree at the same college, so we were there together for a year. For a while I tried to take advantage of having him around. His friends called me "Little Luke" and I was everybody's little buddy, so I had an "in" with the guys. This did nothing but cause the girls to dislike me, so to smooth things over I did two things:

1)   I dropped all but one of my boy pals.

I met A.J. Carpenter during my freshman year. He was part of a group of people on the meal plan who actually liked to hang out in the cafeteria, and my roommate hung with that crowd. Hungry, I followed her to a meal one day, and there he was—the tallest, most athletic, best looking, and most aloof— definitely the pick of the freshman lunch bunch. He had big, brown doe eyes that could make you cry or strip naked (depending on the mood), and hair so wavy it would make you seasick! I zeroed in on him immediately and he introduced himself, but the very next day, he didn't remember me. Or the next, although I did get the *I-know-I-know-you-from-somewhere* look. By the time he noticed how witty, cute, exciting, and fabulous I was (and smart—I slept right next to him in Zoology all semester and got a better grade than he did!), I had had enough of panting after him like a puppy-dog. Eventually, though, we became the best of friends, spending most of our free

18

time together. And several days a week I would allow him to indulge in one of the most intimate, mutually satisfying, simple pleasures concerning myself...

...I had the cleanest hair on campus!

2)   My other *brilliant* plan was to learn to get along with women by jumping right in and pledging a sorority during my junior year at Howard University.

CHAPTER 3

I pledged Sigma Gamma Rho, the youngest, smallest, and most obscure of the four sororities I had to choose from, but the only group that didn't haze or play games requiring "prospectives" to hide their interest in joining. These women, who were mostly educators, didn't have time for cattiness. They had work to do—saving Black children, the Black family and the Black community (preach on)!

Because there were only eleven of us sorority sisters ("sorors") on campus, we had to work extra hard at everything and try to keep up what is called the "Sigma Image." It was difficult, let me tell you! Our mascot is a French poodle—a bitch—so we had our own fun with that, but other peoples' interpolations and misconceptions were hard to deal with. For starters, "Rho" rhymes with "hoe." Enough said. Then, because Sigma Gamma Rho is known for high scholastic achievement, people thought of us as "bookworms." We actually considered that a compliment until nobody but the DJ came to our first two parties. And finally there was the *fat* thing, although only one of us tipped the scales in favor of the so-called "Sigma Weight Requirement."

We were relieved to "cross line," or finish pledging, so that we could get out of each other's hair. Back then, pledgees would live together, dress alike, and actually walk, talk, eat, sleep, and do everything together in a line when we were "on line." All of this was supposed to promote an instant and permanent bond. It did, with six of us: Sheila, Irene, Kern, Joy, Antoinette, and me.

Sheila Staples, the "Short Bitch" at 4'11", had been number one on our line that spring. She was a quick-thinking, tough, perfectly petite little thing from New York. Sheila was not skinny, though; she had some meat on her bones! You know how Stephanie Mills is short, but has a body that won't quit? That's Sheila. With hair down to there and glasses. I liked her because she was attentive, cooperative, smart, and creative. We had worked well together on line, effortlessly vibing off of each other. I'd start with an idea and she'd finish it. Or I could tell her something and weeks later she'd remember every detail of it. Oh, and don't give her a phone number! Once she saw a number scrawled on a scrap of paper in my room and asked, "Where do you think *you're* going?" (The number was for American Airlines.) And one day a friend of mine mentioned that she was interested in adopting a puppy. Sheila rattled off the phone number and address of the local Humane Society.

Sheila knew how to tell a story, too. She would call me, let me talk until I was completely bored with myself, and then drop a bombshell of gossip on me.

"You know one of the Deltas has been dating some white trash drug dealer." Sheila would discuss this piece of information at length, as if that's all there was to it, then feed me a little more information. From then on it would be one surprise after another!

"She started using his drugs and he beat her up."

"They found out she was pregnant when she went to the emergency room."

"The next week she went to have an abortion."

"It turned out she was four months pregnant but didn't know it, and so she couldn't have the abortion."

"So they just decided to elope last week."

"Even though she's not sure he's the father because she can't remember who else she was sleeping with four months ago."

By then I'm laid out on the floor, arms and legs stretched out looking like a big "X"!

At 6'1", Irene Monroe was the "Tall Bitch," number eleven at the end of our line. She was raised in a family of strong, independent, domineering women, and she was just that way. Nothing and no one ever got anything over on her. She was quick to speak up loudly and correct a situation.

Irene's cute, bespectacled baby face with its perfect, white-toothed smile contrasted greatly just below her neck with the largest pair of breasts I have ever had he pleasure of knowing up close and personal. But Irene was never in danger of not being taken seriously, because her stature and close-cropped haircut went a long way to help her get her point across. She was also very smart. Irene had a head full of facts and figures ready to break down to you in the event of a disagreement. She could also argue from a real, practical side of life, having grown up in some projects in New Jersey. Irene would be a terror in a courtroom, but alas, she was choosing the route of a public servant. What else do you do with a History major?

Kern, just plain "Bitch," was number seven on our line. She was a native Washingtonian (so her name wasn't really "Kern," it was "Karen" pronounced all wrong), and a bitch (that native Washingtonian thing again), but she was *real*. She would say exactly what was on her mind, no matter what or to whom. Joy was number two, and we called her "Sigma Gamma *Oh,*" because she was sweet (hence, no bitch name) and curious, but a little slow to think sometimes. Antoinette, number ten, was our pretty, pampered (hence, no bitch name) *"Princess* Gamma Rho."

I was what my sorors called the "Average Bitch," being of average height (5'6") and number six, right in the middle of our pledge line. This particular pet name didn't bother me because I knew that Lynn Joseph was by no means average! I *was* a wishy-washy, middle-of-the-road, *flaky* kind of bitch, though. I found it difficult to make up my mind about most things, even my hair, which I changed every other day (from high school until I pledged and was forced to wear a ponytail under my pledge hat for six weeks).

So, although the extreme togetherness really was good for forming bonds, the *other* five of them (I mean, us)—"The Crew"—just got on our nerves quick! and in the worst way. We had no respect for them because while we overcame our differences in order to work hard and well on line, they didn't get along with each other, let alone with *us*, and tried to pledge part-time, leaving us to pull their weight. With sorority sisters like that, who needed Deltas?

But I digress. *Anyway...*

I met the love of my life at the end of that school year, at the beginning of May, about six weeks after we'd both crossed line. I was in the library writing a term paper when he strolled over, introduced himself with a firm, friendly handshake and just started talking as if I should know who he was (I kinda did). He wasn't what many people would have called attractive, especially on that campus of kings, beauty queens, and a fashion show every week. But that meant *what*? No competition! He was short, skinny, very dark, and he dressed a little corny, but he was smart (rumor: he pulled out a 4.0 while he was on line!), and he had a big, bright, friendly, deep-dimpled smile that crinkled the corners of his eyes (that was some smile!), a cute accent straight out of Africa, and a cool name that rhymed: Nnarami Obawani, or "Rami" (sounds like "mommy") for short. I voted for him for some office of the Greek Council before I had even met him, just because I liked his name.

Me: What do we know about this guy?
Sheila: Which one?
Me: The Alpha with the cool name that rhymes.
Sheila: That's about it.
Me: Okay, put him down.

Shortly after he was elected, Sheila called me after a meeting and said, "Mr. Obawani has expressed a desire for you to be his woman."

"Who?" I asked, instantly annoyed at this person's bold brazenness.

"Nnarami Obawani—the *name* we just voted for last week! He was number five on his line. Remember?"

"I haven't been paying attention."

"Doesn't matter. He's seen you around and heard about you, and he wants you."

"*Please!*"

It was the most ridiculous thing I'd ever heard!

I was so flattered!

We spent four hours talking in the library the day we met, and I got absolutely no work done. Nnarami seemed pretty interested in me and my studies. I went back the next day to finish that paper, but I should have known when I *just happened* to arrive at the same time and *just happened* to sit at the same table that there was no hope—except for me hoping that he would show up, which he did. And even though we talked again for hours, I still couldn't have told you much about him, except that he was indeed smart and had a big, bright, friendly, deep-dimpled smile that crinkled the corners of his eyes (that was some smile!), a cute accent straight out of Africa, and a cool name that rhymed. And that I liked him.

I liked him a lot.

CHAPTER 4

The school year ended a couple of days later, and I was glad! Pledging the sorority that semester was bad enough, but I had made life four times harder for myself because I lived with my brother Luke in suburban Maryland with no car, while working two part-time jobs and attending two different universities. I was having a hard time choosing between being a doctor and a mortician, so I was taking pre-med classes at HU and mortuary science classes at the University of the District of Columbia (UDC). I know it doesn't seem like it, but medicine and funeral service are pretty similar vocations. Either way, you get to put on scrubs, go into an operating room, and perform esoteric procedures on people's bodies!

Luckily Luke and I lived near the subway that had a stop right at UDC. Howard's Law School was across the street from there with shuttle service back to the main campus. So, I would start the day at UDC, then cut my last class short so I could run across the street and catch the shuttle just in time to be late for my first class at Howard.

My waitress job was on the bus line between Howard and home, and my Georgetown library job was at the end of the G2 bus line, which runs rather conveniently between Howard and Georgetown University. I did all of this running around town while I was on line, and people must have thought I was crazy, wearing the same clothes every day and cutting corners like a Nazi!

When school was over, I took a train home to Gary, Indiana for two weeks' vacation. While everyone else is looking for someplace different and exotic to go to unwind, I would rather be no place but home, where I can relax, release, and recharge! At home, where everything is familiar, I can go on autopilot. At home there are people who love me for no reason at all, and they are always happy to see me! Why would anyone ever not want to go home? So during my vacation I intended to soak up all of that love, chill out with my family, show off my new Greek letters, and turn 20 gracefully…but trouble seemed to be brewing from the moment I crossed the city limits.

For one thing, my birthday did not dawn sunny and bright. Rain was pouring down and didn't let up. I ran some errands for my mother while she was at work—a chance to encounter some people and tell them it was my birthday!—and looked forward to my dad, his family and some friends coming over later that evening to celebrate with me.

May 18th is the one day on the calendar that I can call my own, so I always make a big deal out of it. Will and Lorraine, my divorced parents, knew this, but they chose that evening *anyway* to actually *team up* and take turns lambasting me:

> You are so smart that you're *stupid*…
> > We aren't pleased with your *activities*...
> or your indecision about *school*...
> > You aren't "cutting the muster" at *Howard*...
> Move out of your brother's *apartment*...
> > because he's tired of you *leeching* off him...
> You can't make it on your own in *DC*...
> > You can't do all the things you want to *do*…
> You'll have to *sleep with somebody* to get a *job*…
> > or need some *man* to take care of you…
> So just bring your butt back *home*...
> > and go to *Indiana University Northwest*...

which is almost literally on the corner of our street. Now, *that* pissed me off (not that there's anything wrong with IUN), so I called myself running away from home (with my big, grown ass) and left Gary early. An old high school friend, Dina, just happened to be driving back to Delaware State, and offered me a ride.

I didn't go to Luke's apartment when I arrived in the DC area. I had arranged to hide out at Irene's place and let everyone worry for a little while, but when I rolled into town, I couldn't find her new apartment and no one answered her phone. I didn't know where A.J. was living; he roamed around like a gypsy. Nnarami had given me his phone number before I left, and it was still in my purse, so I called and he told me to come right over.

Dina drove to the 14th Street apartment complex where Rami lived. He was waiting outside when we arrived, treating me to that special smile! I introduced them and the three of us quickly unloaded my things, mostly bags of food that my grandmother bought or had cooked and frozen for me. Then I caught Dina making faces behind Nnarami's back.

"Stop it, girl," I spat. "He's nice."

"Good! He just oughta be," Dina said.

"What do you mean by that?"

"Don't tell me you *like* him!"

"What if I do?"

"Like I said, he just *oughta* be!"

When we were done, Rami shook Dina's hand and thanked her for getting me to DC safely. When he turned to go into the building, she made another face.

You see what I mean? about girls?

CHAPTER 5

I don't know what I expected from his living quarters, but maybe because I thought so highly of him I thought Rami would be living like a king in some palatial space.

He lived in one room.

Number 410 was a studio apartment, a simple L-shaped domicile. When you walked in, there was a bathroom immediately on the right. The apartment's one window lay about twenty feet straight ahead. About four paces past the bathroom, turning right, there was a closet in front of you and the kitchen on the left, along the same wall as the window. The kitchen was little more than a wide, shallow niche, with a stove, sink, and refrigerator all lined up in a row inside, with cabinets above and below wherever possible.

The place was sparsely furnished, go figure. In front of the window was a large, rectangular folding table that did duty as a telephone stand / TV table / computer stand / ironing board / dining table / desk. A huge, yellow, sunflower-looking papasan chair worked well as a desk chair / lounge / guest bed. A portable stereo sat on two crates, which were a makeshift headboard for the full-sized mattress sitting on the floor in front of the closet door and across from the kitchen. The only wall decoration was a wooden cassette rack. The mix of music did not give away many clues about the owner of the collection.

We put my food away in his refrigerator, which was nearly empty except for some milk, eggs, some kind of sausage and Gatorade, which again gave away no information about what kind of person Nnarami was. The sport drink was unusual, though, for someone who didn't look like he played sports or worked out. I went to check out the bathroom, and upon seeing the toilet, had to use it. (I think I was potty-trained that way; when I see water, I gotta go!) There was nothing interesting there, either: a black rug…a plain black shower curtain…and a gold naked woman toothbrush with feet!?

I made a mental note to call Irene. Five hours after I made the mental note, however, it was 2:00 am and Nnarami and I were still up talking about... about... everything and nothing in particular, just like at the library. Well, I actually told him my entire life story, and he amused me with a tall tale about this huge family that he supposedly had back in Boise, Idaho. *Right.* The big family part, okay, but who lives in Boise? *Idaho?* Again, though, I was thrown because what he was telling me did not fit the image I had of him and whatever his family should be like. Divorces and stepfamilies were too *common*, and not what I had in mind. He didn't talk about his dad at all, but his mom was regular old Betty Williams from Arkansas, who later changed her name to Khadijah, moved to Mogadishu, Somalia, and became the first wife (of six, total) of some radical politician there.

So with all of this information in one ear and out the other (it just did not compute!), I finally fell asleep fully clothed on the mattress, and Rami slept in the papasan in front of the TV.

CHAPTER 6

"Can you cook?" he asked me the next morning.

"What? You mean breakfast?" I asked.

"I'd like some pancakes. Do you know how to make them?"

I didn't imagine he would eat anything as plain as pancakes. I would have thought something more exotic like crêpes, maybe, but there he was, holding a box of Aunt Jemima Buttermilk Complete.

"Not at all," I replied. "Can you?"

"No," he said, which left me wondering what he usually did with the mix…

"Well then, I'll give it my best shot."

I made two embarrassing splatter-batterdisks and had just remembered the rule (but not where it came from) that "the first two are for the trash," when Nnarami stepped into the kitchen, shook his head, and nicely ordered me out.

"Go," he said, taking the spatula and pan away from me.

"But the first two are always for the trash," I protested, stepping back into the big room—that's relative, of course, to the casket-sized kitchen. But I dared not protest too much, and quickly settled into the papasan.

6-6-7... I began dialing Irene's number, then remembered my manners. "May I use your phone?" I yelled. ...9-1-5-9.

"Sure. Go on!" Nnarami yelled back over much banging and scraping. What was he doing? As far as I knew, pancake preparation had always been a quiet kind of thing, but he was tearing something up in there!

"Hello?"

"Hey, Irene. Where you been, girl?"

"Lynn?! What do you MEAN, 'WHERE YOU BEEN?' WHERE ARE YOU!? YOU WERE SUPPOSED TO BE HERE YES-ter-daaaaaay!" Irene's yelling tapered to a whine as her system flooded with relief enzymes, if there are such things.

"Whoaaa!" I laughed. "I'm at Nnarami's place."

"Obawani?"

"Yeah."

"I didn't know you knew him that well."

"Just from those coupla days at the library—remember I told you?"

"Oh, yeah. Where does he live?"

"On 14th and Harvard. Where exactly is your place?"

"1629 Irving, Lynn, like I told you."

"Oh yeah! Well, when I couldn't find you and my ride had to go, I called Nnarami and he let me come over."

"So you spent the night there?"

"Yeah. We were so busy talking that I forgot to try calling you back."

"Talking, huh?"

I had to pull Irene back from the conclusion she had jumped to. "Yes, talking. It's not like that," I half whispered, needlessly. It was tight in Rami's apartment, but there was that remarkable din still coming from the kitchen.

"I didn't mean anything. He's pretty cool, isn't he?"

"Yeah, he's real nice."

"Good, girl. So when will you be here?"

"How about later this afternoon? I'll give you a call, all right?" *Crash, bang!* from the kitchen. "I think we're about to have breakfast."

I gave her Rami's number and hung up just as he came out of the kitchen. After all that banging and scraping, there he was flourishing a plate that could have been photographed for the cover of an IHOP menu. And it tasted every bit as good, too. Go figure!

It was a hot and hazy Saturday, so we spent the day loafing. Rami showed me pictures that he took in Egypt. I wondered if he had been born in Africa, just lived there for a while, only visited from time to time… It was wild seeing pictures of the pyramids and sphinxes that weren't in a textbook, National Geographic, or on public television. These objects were important, awesome, and larger than life, but Rami's pictures made them seem intimate and familiar at the same time. It was like picking up somebody's family photo album and seeing a picture of Jesus at age 12, in his pajamas, opening Christmas presents in the living room.

Rami also showed me a photo of his mother. She was exquisitely beautiful. She looked like Sarah Vaughan, the songstress, when she was young. Look her up in a dictionary; a good one will have her picture, and you'll see what I'm saying.

There was nothing on TV, so we turned on the radio and sang along to some of the best hits and oldies on my favorite station. I was surprised Rami knew them.

He met Marmalade
Down in old New Orleans,
Struttin' her stuff on the street.
She said, "Hello, hey Joe—
You wanna give it a go?"
Um-hmm
Geechee, geechee, ya ya, da da...

He didn't sing very well, but he sang with gusto! I was glad because I love to sing, but I'm no Whitney Houston, either.

Later, we walked down Harvard Street to Jimmy's Seafood & Carryout for lunch. After pigging out on chicken wings and white bread with mambo sauce (I was shocked again by his choice of eateries as well as his choice of food), we went to the Safeway so that I could pick up some diet fare. I selected a can of chocolate Slim-Fast shake mix and some Lean Cuisine meals.

"You don't need that," he said, taking the stuff from me and setting it all in a freezer.

"Yes, I do," I said, picking the items back up and scurrying over to the checkout, hugging the packages to my chest. "I'm going on a diet."

"You don't need to diet. You look fine."

"Thanks! *Anyway*..."

The cashier rang up my purchases as I fumbled around in my purse for my last $20 in the world. I slapped it onto the cashier's open hand before she could take the bill that Nnarami was handing to her. Then I wished I hadn't been so quick and stubborn about it, lest he not try to pick up the tab when my money actually ran out.

We went back to Rami's apartment, called Irene, and took my things over to her apartment. With so many bags to carry, Rami took the carrying strap from a gym bag of his, and attached it to several of mine to make it a little easier.

I whipped up a Slim-Fast shake for my dinner while Rami and Irene bonded over a discussion of the pathos that made a well-proportioned young woman want to diet. They needn't have worried; not ten minutes later I put a Lean Cuisine in the microwave.

The two of them, my co-hosts, were hitting it off really well and had moved on to the less serious topic of which of our sorors and frat brothers should date each other.

"I think I like Derrick," Irene announced.

Nnarami was delighted. Apparently he and Derrick were close. "That's good stuff! I'll hook you two up!"

"Which one is he again?" I asked.

"My sands," Rami said. A "sands" is anyone who pledged at the same time you did, particularly if it was the same fraternity or sorority ("to cross the burning sands into the land of *sorority/fraternity name here*").

"Number eleven," explained Irene. We knew all of our sands better by their numbers because for six long weeks that was how we identified each other before we actually met and learned names. Irene had been number eleven on our line, at the end just like Derrick. Being somebody's "number" was a good reason to strike up a friendship with that person, to be "spec's." "Spec," pronounced "spesh," is short for "special" and denotes just that—a special relationship.

"Oh, the tall one! Yeah, he's cool." While most of Rami's line brothers tended to be stand-offish, Derrick always went out of his way to be cordial. I was embarrassed that whenever I saw him, I'd invariably give him the dreaded *I-know-I-know-you-from-somewhere* look. He'd go, "Hey, *sands*," and I'd remember.

"That would be cute, wouldn't it? The end of our line dating the end of their line," Irene laughed.

"Who was number five on your line?" Rami asked.

"Euwwww...Darleeeene!" Irene and I said in unison. Our number five was one of "The Crew."

"I suppose that means I wouldn't like her," Rami guessed.

"No, and I don't like my number on your line, either," I told him. Their number six was phony and a snob.

"Well, let's just forget about them and be each other's spec's," Rami suggested. "Number five and Number six."

"Okay," I agreed, and we hugged. I was pleased with my new spec!

We ordered a pizza (my third dinner that evening, are you counting?) and watched TV and talked late into the night. Around 11:00 pm, Irene got tired of us and politely put us out.

"You guys have got to go if you're going to stay up talking. I need to go to bed," she said. Irene's apartment was an efficiency as well, so we were sitting in her dining area, which widened into her living/sleeping quarters.

"Awww, maaan. Okay. Rami, I'll walk you downstairs," I said, pouting.

"Why don't you just go with him?"

Well—just so you know—I'm highly suggestible, so I did.

CHAPTER 7

I couldn't deny the attraction between Nnarami and me, but don't get me wrong—it wasn't the physical or even the chemical kind. I didn't get all funny and googly-eyed; I just wanted to be around him. This was like one of those crushes boys and girls have on each other back in grade school that make them chase each other around the playground and crawl through the mud!

I thought about it: *Here is this really smart guy, but that makes him a nerd. He wears dress slacks and shirts and ties all the time, which makes him square. His build is not even remotely athletic, and he doesn't wear a "fade"* (the latest haircut back then), *which makes him...I don't know...a nerd again. He's only a neophyte* (a new member of a fraternity or sorority), *and he isn't popular...* Back in grade school, though, none of those things mattered. Everybody was scrawny, some were missing teeth, nobody was really smart or really dumb just yet, and you didn't have a choice about your clothes or hair because your mama took care of that. I decided to do away with any criteria and just enjoy my school girl crush.

When we got back to his place, Rami turned on the radio, dimmed the lights (a dimmer!?), and we chilled out on our backs across the mattress with our feet up on the wall.

"You need new tennis shoes," he told me.

I kicked off my dirty, torn Tretorns. My toes were poking out of holes in the sides, and I had never put them all the way on, just walked on the backs of them so that they slid on and off like sandals.

"Why don't you get some new ones?" Rami asked.

"S'not time yet," I mocked. "You don't even start wearing them out in public until they look like this. It's the style, don't you know?" He just looked at me. It really *was* the style— a decade earlier, and in those preppy white teen magazines my mother used to make me read.

"Okay, I can't afford any," I confessed, and changed the subject. "How'd you get those scars on your knees? They look terrible."

"I can't tell you, because then I would have to kill you."

"So tell me and kill me quick."

"Why do you have those stretch marks on *your* knees?"

"Because I suddenly gained a whole lot of weight in high school and didn't grow into it until two years later."

Nnarami seemed concerned. "Do you take care of them?"

"There's nothing I can do. They're not going anywhere."

He did a cool backward roll off the bed since I was blocking him in on his left and the radio was on his right. Rami went around the corner into the bathroom, and came back with a stick of cocoa butter. "Here, let me do this for you," and he rubbed the cocoa butter into the skin on the insides of my knees, which tickled me so much I couldn't stand it!

"Stop!" I yelled, laughing.

"Why? What's wrong?"

"That tickles!"

"This?" he asked, swiping my knees with the stick. I jerked away from him to the left and hit the closet door.

"Yes, that! I'm extremely ticklish! Hey, give me that thing!"

I showed him how he could apply the cocoa butter without tickling me and when he finished, we resumed our feet-up-on-the-wall position on the bed.

"Do you have a boyfriend?" he asked.

"Nope. Oh, wait a minute! There's A.J., but he's not my boyfriend, though."

"What is he, then?"

"I guess he's my best friend, except he's a boy. We're cosmically linked."

"I see."

"So…you got a girlfriend?"

"Tell me more about this A.J."

"There's really not much to tell. I've known him since freshman year. It used to be a bunch of us hanging out. Anyway, he's tall, nice, funny, and pretty smart…"

"Is he good-looking?"

"Well, yeah." *Fine as hell was more like it.*

"If he isn't your boyfriend, why don't you have one?" He sure was being nosey—and evasive. I didn't like him always answering my questions with questions of his own. I knew so little about him!

"I don't know," I said. "I guess I haven't had time. You know, being on line and everything."

"So you mean you weren't with anybody all that time?"

"Well, I won't say all *that*," I half-admitted. Just like the frats had "sweethearts" who helped the pledgees with their various projects and "morale" while they were on line, sororities had male "sweethearts." I don't know for sure exactly what the girls did for the guys, but our aptly named "Rhomeos" were multi-purpose!

"Have you slept with anybody since then?"

I might have been offended if I had something to admit, but I didn't.

"No." I tried again: "How about you?"

"A grad student named Tracy."

"Oh." *Fine time for him to answer me!*

"Do you want a boyfriend?"

"…desires you to be his woman…"

Aaaah, shit.

"I don't know. I haven't thought much about it."

"You need somebody to take care of you."

"What I need is a job so I can get my own apartment," I sighed, thinking for the first time since I'd returned to D.C. about the rock and the hard place I was between: on the lam with no income and no place to call my own. This was not a good situation for a Taurus person, for whom *money, stuff,* and *territory* are chief concerns. "Maybe I should just quit tripping and move back with my brother."

"I can tell you three reasons why that would be a bad idea," Rami said without hesitation. "1—it's too far from school; 2—it's too far from me; and 3—it's too close to Lee."

I blinked and my mouth dropped open. Lee was an older Alpha, and just before I pledged we had a fling that we shouldn't have had. He wasn't my boyfriend or anything, so embarrassment and Sigma Image kept me from mentioning it to anybody. I had expected that Lee would keep his mouth shut, too.

"Okaaaay…"

"May I have a kiss?" he asked, turning towards me.

Here we go…

He'd been so nice…

Aaah, what could it hurt?

I let him.

I like first kisses. They're usually pretty exciting, once you settle into each other's rhythm and figure out whose nose and teeth and tongue and hands are going to go where. Ten seconds later we had that all settled, and I knew exactly where this episode was headed: *nowhere.* I wasn't about to lead him on, so I gently pulled away.

Even in the dim light I could see the confusion written all over his face. "Don't you want to make love with me?"

"*Huh?*" I didn't mean to say it out loud, but how did he figure...? I mean, we should have still been negotiating the kissing!

"Don't you want me?"

No.

"Ahh...sure," I said, not being one to tread on anyone's feelings. "But don't you think it's kinda soon?"

"You like me, don't you?"

"Yeah..."

"Then it's okay. Make love with me."

"All right," I mumbled. (Somebody somewhere should be discussing *this* pathos!)

Nnarami smiled. He was such a cutie when he did that! He crawled over me to fumble around in the closet for a minute, then turned the lights all the way off and got back on the bed. After much pulling, tugging, and snapping of latex (that was the trouble before we discovered *MAGNUM* brand!), Nnarami worked his way—the rest of the way—into my heart.

It must be that my "heart" is whatever organ is three feet high on my body. In nursery school, I did a lot of kissing when my lips were three feet high. In grade school, I had lots of secret crushes when the middle of my chest (my actual, physical heart) was at three feet. In high school, I gained a lot of weight from my love affair with food when my stomach was at the three-foot mark. And now it seemed the seat of my emotions was situated squarely in my lap, not too far from the seat of my pants!

For three days Nnarami and I lived a most hedonistic existence, only leaving the apartment to run to Jimmy's for food that would sit on the table for hours before we got around to eating it. Because the apartment was so small, we were able to do most everything from the bed, which we hardly ever vacated. Rami blamed me for it:

"You're bad," he said. I put my index fingers up on either side of my head and showed him my "horns" with a devilish little grin to match.

"Takes one to know one," I reminded him, so Rami showed me his horns, too. But apparently, he was *so* bad that he used not just two fingers, but both his arms and hands!

During those looong days and short nights at Rami's, sometimes we talked. When we got tired of talking, we wrote notes back and forth.

> Hi.
> Hello.
> How are you?
> Hot.
> Oh, yeah? (smile)
> Yes, it's getting HOT in here.
> Well, welcome to the Hut...

Whenever the messages became suggestive...well, I already told you how suggestible I am.

> *You are my favorite lady*
> *And you are my favorite man, yes you are*
> *So it feels good to know that you feel the same way*
> *And forever and a day*
> *Together we will be*
> *Nothing on this earth could ever*
> *Take you away from me*
> *'Cause I've been kissed, but I—*
> *Never knew love like this!*
> *And I've been missed, but I—*
> *Never knew love like this!*

Loved someone before, but I—
(Never knew love)
I've had lots of lovin'
But I never knew love like this!

…all out of tune, but this one was our favorite song.

CHAPTER 8

I never did make it to Irene's. On Wednesday, I went over there to pick up a few things and felt so bad that I was basically using her place for storage, that I insisted on spending the night there with my stuff. Nnarami was at the door to collect me first thing the next morning.

After depositing me in his apartment, Rami grabbed his suit jacket and headed out the door, announcing that he would be gone for most of the day. I didn't ask any questions.

I sat around for an hour or so before I finally wondered what I should be doing. Having sex with Rami was all that came to mind. Couldn't do that, so I rummaged around in one of my bags and pulled out some art supplies. I'm not particularly artistic, but I had an idea and was starting a hand painted T-shirt business. I painted a T-shirt for Rami. It had pyramids laid out in the shape of his fraternity letters and "1906," the year it was founded, on the back.

After painting the shirt and then watching TV for another two hours, I called Irene.

"A.J. just stopped by looking for you," she said, and I realized I hadn't spoken to him since before I left for home. Suddenly, I missed him. "I wouldn't tell him where you were, and he seemed a little miffed, but he left a number for you to call him."

I chuckled, imagining for a moment the eyes-rolled-up, pursed-lipped, exasperated look on A.J.'s face when Irene refused to disclose my whereabouts. He would *not* be fond of her after that!

"Rami's gone," I announced.

44

"Where? What happened?!"

"He just went somewhere for the day."

"Oh. Well, where would he go? He's not working, he's not in school..." Irene speculated.

"That's what I was wondering," I said.

"You didn't ask?"

"Nope. I never ask him about anything."

"Well, if it wasn't important enough for you to ask, then there's no sense in worrying about it. And anyway, he's nice. You ain't gotta worry about him. But I know you miss him," Irene teased, knowing our daily routine. "I gotta go…"

I called A.J. and brought him up to speed about the last two weeks of my life.

"So, I'm not doing anything, am I? Just like my mother and father said."

"No, you're not, Lynn. You're over there being all in love and that's nice and everything, and it's only been a few days, but you *do* need to get yourself together. This is fine for now, but do you think this Rami is the type of guy who wants a woman that just sits around? He sounds too smart for that! And I don't know—maybe he can *afford* to keep you, but please!"

"You're right. So I need to get a job, huh? And move out."

"Do you know where you're going to?"

"I—"

"Do you like the things that life is showing you?"

I howled! He was sing/saying Diana Ross' *Theme from Mahogany*. I should have known what was up when he ended that first sentence with a preposition!

"Do you know? But seriously," A.J. continued. "Yeah, you should get a job, but school is almost out so all the high school kids are looking for jobs, too. What about one of your old gigs?" he suggested.

I was lucky. One phone call is all it took, and by the time Rami returned early that evening, I had reclaimed my old waitressing job, beginning the next day. He didn't seem to understand why I wanted to work.

"I really need the money. I gotta have enough to get registered for school in August."

"You could ask *me*. I get upset when you don't ask me for things."

"I can't ask you for something like that," I protested.

"Why not? You deserve to be treated well."

"Hmm. Anyway, it'll be nice to get out."

"Aren't you happy being here with me?"

"Yes, but I've got to *do* something." Besides, getting away and going to work gave me time to recuperate from our all-day-and-half-the-night indoor sporting activities. I thought my body would have adjusted to his size and been used to him by then, but maybe because he made love like he made pancakes, or maybe because we hadn't let up *at all*, the sex was still excruciating.

Oh! I'm sorry…

Were you thinking it was all beautiful, romantic and sexy?

CHAPTER 9

Granted—A.J. had an *uncanny* ability to sniff me out no matter where I might be, but once he found me, I knew others wouldn't be far behind.

Robert was one of my friends from Gary who was also doing time on the East Coast, at a nearby military college in Virginia— the same one my brother Bill had attended. He called Luke's place on Friday looking for me, but I had been "missing" for a week. Luke called Irene, as A.J. had thought to do. All she told him was that she could get in touch with me, so Luke just gave Robert her number. I knew it wouldn't be long before one of my parents would be calling, too.

Robert phoned. He told Irene that he was coming to DC that night and wanted to see me. Rami and I were on our way to his frat brother's house for a party, but we stopped at Irene's first so that I could see my friend.

Robert and another cadet were sitting on Irene's couch drinking wine when we arrived. Maybe the wine was the reason, but it was easy to tell that Robert was not himself that evening. We had always been just friends—*truly*—however, he came out of his face with a bunch of madness, the likes of which I had never heard from him before.

"Lynn, baby!" he slurred as Rami and I entered the apartment. "Come 'ere, giiirl! Gimme a hug."

I went to give him a quick hug, but Robert held on and then let his hands slip down towards my behind. I laughed it off, grabbed his hands, and twisted away from him like we were dancing or something. Out of the corner of my eye, it didn't look as if Rami had seen that. He was busy settling into a place on the floor near the door to the bathroom. I squeezed past Robert and sat between him and his friend on the couch.

"Man, I told Jamie you was fine. Giiirl, you lookin' good!"

"Thanks. Nice to meet you, Jamie." I noted that Jamie looked like a grown-up Sammy Walker.

"So, Robert…how's school?" I said, trying to get the conversation back on track. Jamie was smart; he was busy keeping an uneasy eye on my boyfriend. Irene was in the kitchen, cleaning up. She came out shortly, though, sat across the room on the floor and talked with Rami.

"It's cool, baby."

"Good. So what's up?" I asked, punching him in the arm, an action usually guaranteed to put a guy in "buddy" mode. But then I made the mistake of picking up his uniform hat off the coffee table and trying it on.

"You know what it means when you put on the hat."

I did remember; when you put on a cadet's hat, it was supposed to mean that you intended to sleep with him. Since that was a non-issue with us, wearing his hat had never been an issue, either. I had tried it on many times before. This time, I put the hat back on the table.

"Naw, go ahead—wear it," Robert said, trying to put the hat back on me. "But you know what you gotta do."

I ducked from under the hat, took it from him, and handed it to Jamie, who seemed happy and relieved to take the hat out of play before Rami saw what was going on.

I tried one last time to defuse Robert. "Hey, how's your girlfriend?"

"That's what I came to ask you about."

"Ask *me*? About *her*?" She was from Gary, so she was cool, but I had only seen her once or twice.

"No, not really *about* her. See, we got this big dance coming up next week, and she just flaked on me. She can't come, man."

"Aw, that's too bad."

"I got the tickets already, so I'm stuck with 'em. I wanted to know if you would go with me, man. She said you cool, it would be okay with her."

"Oh, sure! I mean, let me see." I leaned past Jamie (he sure did smell good!) to look over at Rami, who was now glaring in Robert's direction. "What do you think—can I?"

"It's time for us to go," he said, getting up.

Meanwhile, Robert…I swear, that black boy paled like old charcoal! And his eyebrows were raised all the way to the ceiling. He picked up his keys and his hat, dropped them, picked them up again…

"All right then, Lynn. I'll, uh, call you next week," he said as he hurried to get up and out of Irene's apartment. We all stood up. "Thanks, Irene. Nice meeting you, ah…"

"Yeah, sure," Rami said from the hallway already.

Irene's door was weighted, so it closed automatically behind him. In the two seconds before he opened it for the rest of us to walk out, Robert whispered, "I didn't know that was your man! I thought he was here to see Irene!"

"Come *on*, Lynn," Rami demanded when Robert opened the door.

"All right. I'm just saying—"

"*Now.*"

?

"Call me here on Tuesday night," I told Robert. "Nice to meet you, Jamie!"

I ran down the hallway to the elevator that Rami was holding for me. He pushed a button, and the doors closed just as Robert and Jamie reached them.

The frat party that night was…a party for the frat. Those self-absorbed guys didn't need anybody else to be there. I didn't dance or anything, just spent the entire night tagging along behind Rami, who apparently had developed a taste for ordering me around:

"Lynn, sit there."
"Lynn, come here."
"Wait for me."
"Follow me."
"Lynn, *jump*." (just kidding!)

How high? hee hee!

On Saturday, Irene got a call from my *play* grandmother, Hattie (an elderly friend of my mother's), who lived in DC. She said there was an important-looking letter for me at her house, which was on the bus route to my job, so I picked it up on the way there.

I deduced that Hattie was just trying to get me over to her house to say her piece about me running away and breaking my mother's heart, because the "important-looking letter" was really only junk mail—something about a pre-med scholars program that was to begin in two weeks. Somebody obviously made a mistake, because I hadn't applied to anything.

I missed Rami when I went to work. Rami missed me, too. Every day when I got home, there was some little gift waiting for me: blue and gold barrettes (Sigma colors) for my hair on Thursday, my favorite candy on Friday, and on Saturday, a gold naked man toothbrush with feet!

A.J. had dinner at the restaurant at the end of my shift on Sunday, so he treated me to a cab ride home to Irene's. I accepted the ride without even considering if it was out of his way. I still did not know where he was living.

I called Nnarami from Irene's apartment and he came over to get me. He had this beautifully wrapped box. I took it from him graciously, then ripped the paper off like a madwoman.

In my glee, I forgot to introduce A.J. and Rami, but they took care of that themselves.

"So *you're* Rami."

"And *you're* A.J." Just then I looked up and caught Rami smiling (!) at A.J., and A.J. smiling back! They shook hands. That usually didn't happen. Usually the guys I dated (and I use that term loosely) were okay about A.J. because he sounds imaginary (like my own personal "Jiminy Cricket") or they thought he was my gay friend or something. But then the guy would get a *look* at A.J., and all that understanding ceased! He'd stand there and grit on A.J., and A.J. would look at me funny, like I shoulda told the guy something! Well, I never figured out what would be appropriate to say. So we would beat a hasty retreat (leave in a hurry) and then the guy would say:

"He does all this stuff for you and he looks like *that*, and you never—you're not fucking him?"

"No."

"Shit. *I* would."

It always happened that way, except for this time.

"I'm sorry! Rami, A.J...Rami," I introduced, sweeping one hand back and forth as if to point out who was who. Then it was back to work on the box!, which was taped shut on all four sides.

"Yes, you're rude, but you're forgiven," A.J. chided me. Then to Rami, "So, what's in the box?"

"Tennis shoes."

"Bless you."

CHAPTER 10

On Tuesday, I ended up hanging around after work, intrigued by some of my male co-workers, who were having a discussion about women and dating. They noticed me standing around, but thankfully did not pull me into the conversation.

Brian was saying, "...and I mean, this honey looked so good, she could have anybody she wanted! Didn't she, Mark? I'd even drink her bath water!"

And then Mark said, "Yeah, but why she hook up wit' that ugly dude, though?"

I couldn't deny the attraction between Nnarami and me, but don't get me wrong—it wasn't the physical or even the chemical kind.

"That's 'cause he gon' give her everything she want, so he can hold on to her," Larry chimed in on his way back to the kitchen.

"You deserve to be treated well."

"Oh, I got what she want," leered Brian, motioning towards his crotch.

"Nigga, he ain't talkin' 'bout that! He talkin' 'bout you gotta be payin' some bills, buyin' some jewelry...man, you still livin' in yo grandmama's basement!"

"I get upset when you don't ask me for things."

"All right. Yeah, okay. But you know what? She takin' that nigga's money, but when he ain't looking, you know that honey steppin' out wit' a fine brother like me, ya dig? Gettin' out on that nigga, ha-haaa! *Creep, creep!*" Mark sang, doing a little slow-grind dance with himself.

Just then the door opened and Nnarami strolled in. There hadn't been much traffic in the restaurant that evening, so both guys got up to either seat or serve what they thought was a new customer. They stopped short and stared, however, when Rami did not even hesitate at the "Please Wait to be Seated" sign. He walked straight over to me, and putting his hands on either side of my face, kissed me slowly and sensuously as he pulled me off my perch on a low partition wall.

"Come on, baby. We're going out," he said, and without waiting for a comment, he turned and walked back out the door. I was dazed for a few seconds, but then I snatched my jacket from behind the wall and fairly flew out of there after him, forgetting to check the expressions on my co-worker's faces.

The next day, Wednesday, was my day off, and that night was the dance at Virginia Military College. My dress was at Irene's, so I went over there to get ready. She was gone, so I let myself in with the spare key she had given me. Rami was upset that I was still going to go out with Robert, but I guess I convinced him that Robert was really okay, so he came over to Irene's with me to "help."

Rami let me get dressed, but kept ruining my hair. Before then, he had only seen it in that pledge ponytail (so neat and easy that for once, I stuck with one hairstyle), hanging out from under the purple bandana that I had taken a fancy to. He marveled with his hands at the cascades of curls that I made with the curling iron ("That's good stuff!"), and he waited for me to return that night so he could mess it up again with a pillow and some sheets.

That Friday marked two weeks since I had left home. Irene called to tell me that I had been "caught," that a letter from my mother had arrived for me at her apartment. I felt a tingle in my armpits. I had no desire to be in contact with her or my father until I had done something with myself to prove them wrong.

So far, I hadn't done a thing. In fact, I was actually living up to their sad predictions: I was not making any decisions about school, I was not on my own, I was allowing a man to take care of me…and already I had gotten two dunning calls from creditors at my job.

I pulled out and carefully re-read the erroneous instructions I had received to attend the South Carolina Science Scholars Seminar (SC-SSS), two months of classes all day long in six areas that would prepare the participants to take the Medical College Admissions Test (MCAT) and introduce them to the rigors of a medical school curriculum. I wasn't sure that I was still med-school bound, but it couldn't hurt. If I did well, I could throw that in Lorraine and Will's faces. And for a while I could forget about trying to take care of myself because not only would the program pay for transportation, but room and board was also free for the two months.

SC-SSS participants were required to arrive in one week.

For a couple of days I agonized over the decision to leave Nnarami while I rushed to get all the necessary paperwork together, anyway.

Nnarami asked me to call him while I was away. I called once. He asked me to write to him. I didn't. He asked me not to cut my hair. I cut it. I heard from Irene that he left DC about a week after I did to spend the summer laying out on the beaches of Jamaica. She told me that he missed me terribly and that he'd wanted to ask me to stay, but A.J. had advised him against it:

"Her mind's made up, and she doesn't work well with

ultimatums, so I wouldn't try that if I were you."

What somebody should have advised him against was buying me those tennis shoes, because you know what they say: Buy somebody a pair of shoes and they'll walk right out of your life in them.

I don't know why I didn't call or write, because I missed him, too. But I assumed we'd just pick up where we left off when I returned in the fall.

CHAPTER 11

I hitched a ride with an SC-SSS participant from Baltimore who was driving to South Carolina. The program paid for transportation, but you had to get there first and be reimbursed. Seeing as I only had $8 to my name, driving was my only option. Carla Jones, if she was taken aback by a total stranger calling *("You don't know me, but…")* and bumming a six-hour ride, was as cool as she could be. Cold, even.

"How much stuff you got?" Carla asked, after having me twice explain who I was and exactly how I had gotten her telephone number (from an SC-SSS secretary). Her voice was soft and feminine, and would have been comforting except she clipped her words and phrases in order to sound terse, hard and tough. Carla sounded something like Halle Berry trying to play a crackhead.

"Just one duffel bag and another small bag."

"Oh." Long pause. "Be ready to leave on Saturday night. I'll be to DC to get you at 8:00."

"I don't get off work until 11:00, so could we make it later?"

"Listen, I don't—"

"N-never mind. That's fine. I don't have to work that day." I had to quit sometime, I supposed.

"That's *right*." Then I heard her grumbling.

"What did you say?" I asked.

"Nothing. Be ready at 8:00. You only got one bag. *Right?*"

"Yes, and another small one." Carla sighed loudly and then got directions to Irene's place. I didn't want to try to leave from Rami's because I might have changed my mind, so he came over to Irene's and waited for Carla with me. We didn't talk much. He gave me another gift: a keychain that said, "My Man Is An Alpha." I didn't have any keys to put on it. He told me to call and to write to him. And not to cut my hair. I said okay.

Carla arrived in a huge, old, bright-orange Volvo. She was leaning her tall, slender frame against the car, arms folded across her chest with the trunk open, when Rami and I came downstairs at 2:00 am (she changed the time). Her hair was an unremarkable brown, just past shoulder-length, thick and beautiful, the edges curving slightly into her face. Carla looked Native American. She had sharp, aquiline features and eyes that looked wise, but hard and tired. Her eyes and her personality seemed to match that car perfectly—except for the color. I couldn't see the bright orange in her anywhere.

"Lynn Joseph," she presumed, unfolding one arm and extending her hand.
"Yeah, hi." We shook hands. She had a firm grip, so at least I knew she was real. I can't stand a limp-wristed handshake, and try to steer clear of people who give them. By definition a handshake is a *grasp,* and these people either don't know that or simply don't want to do it. Usually these are the same people who don't have anything going on with themselves...or at the very least, they're showing that they don't give a damn about meeting you.
"Carla Jones, Nnarami Obawani. Nnarami, Carla." I felt funny introducing them—this total stranger to my Virtual Stranger.
Rami and I had already said good-bye inside. I didn't think it was the kind of display Miss Jones needed to see. So he and I hugged for a moment, and I climbed into the car.
"Good-bye and good luck," Rami said.
"Thanks. See ya!"

Rami walked away from Irene's apartment building slowly, backwards, watching us drive down the street. Then he turned and headed for home the right way, walking that walk of his, where those bony but broad shoulders turned this way and that, swinging his arms and seeming to give his legs momentum. He walked like Arnold Schwarzenegger—the walk of a much larger man. But somehow Rami's slight stature didn't fool me for one minute. Somehow I figured that there was easily much more to him than I would ever know.

CHAPTER 12

To say that I was uneasy looking forward to the long drive with this beautiful but strange woman was an understatement. You've probably seen enough movies to understand how I felt about a person such as Carla Jones— *"Fatal Attraction," "Single White Female," "Basic Instinct," "A Thin Line Between Love and Hate…"*

The car comforted me in an odd sort of way. The roomy leather seat was cold and hard, and the car had the strong gasoline smell that Volkswagens tend to have. I breathed deeply and looked around. The ashtray was open and full of change and a little marble horse. The radio was new to the car, and it was working, but there were all kinds of wires hanging out of it. There was nothing else interesting in the front seat, and the rest of the vehicle was spotless.

Unsure of how I was going to make it all the way to South Carolina with this woman, I took the easy route and tried to sleep most of the way. I thought she'd be happy not to have to make conversation, but instead I think it pissed her off. One time I woke up and peeked at her, and she was scowling and muttering to herself as she drove. Then when Carla stopped for gas and saw that I was awake, she asked me for money.

"I don't have any money—just $8—but I can give you $4." I held out four bills. "That's why I had to drive. Hitch a ride, I mean." She had this incredulous look on her face for a second—eyes wide and jaw a little slack—then snatched the money from me and walked away grumbling. I went back to sleep. I thought that was best.

The next time I woke up was because we had arrived at the SC State campus. The sun on my face, the noise from Carla slamming her door when she got out, and the vibrations from her unloading her bags from the trunk rousted me from my slumber. I jumped out of the car a little disoriented, but just in time to grab my two bags before Carla closed the trunk.

She walked ahead of me into the dorm. At the front desk, Carla looked at the program roster and saw an old friend's name.

"Oh! I see Michelle Wilson is here. I'll room with her," she announced. I was a little hurt that she didn't even consider having me as her roommate. Sure, I'd pissed her off, but other than that, I thought we were getting along fine!

"I'm sorry, honey," said the front desk woman. "Everyone else is already here. The two of you will have to room together." I took the key she offered and promptly put it on my "Alpha" keychain. I felt a little sorry for Carla, but a little smug at the same time. She stared at the woman for a few seconds, then at the list, then at me. I shrugged my shoulders like, "I don't know."

The check-in lady was waiting. "Well?" she asked.

"Fine," Carla told her, snatching the other key off the counter and picking up her bags. And to me, "Let's go."

Our room was unusually large, as rooms at the end of a hallway tend to be. On the corner, the room had windows on two sides, making it not only roomy, but bright as well. Cheery it was not, at least not until Carla got through with it.

The first thing Carla did when she saw the triple bunk bed was claim the best one for herself. The top bunk was too high (there was no ladder), but the middle one was just right. She swung her lithe body up onto it by way of the heating unit in front of a window, and just sat there for a few minutes, watching me. I got the feeling she was marking her territory, so I peeked in the closets, the dresser drawers, and checked out the views from all of the windows before I walked over and put my bags on the lower bunk. It looked like too much trouble to climb up top, but on the other hand, the lower bunk was close enough to the ground to make one feel, well, *lowly*.

I had wisely packed a couple of Lorraine's sheets and my "desert sunset and sand dunes" comforter. I had the whole ensemble on the bed in about sixty seconds, but Carla had come with the BIG picture in mind. She hopped down, dragged the mattress off her bunk, and pulled a can of Lysol out of one bag.

"Mattresses are so personal," she explained, spraying it on both sides. "It's almost like sleeping with somebody." After allowing it to dry for a few minutes while she sprayed the dresser drawers, Carla returned the mattress to the bunk and then made up her bed. She had brought two extra pillows and an entire sheet and comforter set, complete with pillow shams and a dust ruffle—all in pink satin. Her bunk was fit for a princess. She acted like it.

A floor lamp seemed to give Carla a brilliant idea. She plugged it in, turned it on and off, and said, "Come on."

"Where're we going?" I asked.

"To scout out some more furniture."

On the way down the motel-like, open-air hallway, Carla tried doors and we peeked inside a couple of rooms that were not locked. Seems our bunk bed and that floor lamp were unusual accoutrements for rooms in this dorm.

In the basement, we hit the jackpot—exercise equipment ("*Here's our gym*") and lounge furniture, lots of it.

"Should we take a whole couch or just a couple of those fluffy chairs?" Carla asked me. I was shocked that she would let me venture an opinion.

"Two chairs, at least until we get to know the other people in the program. People get comfortable on couches and want to stay. They won't lounge as much in the chairs."

"Good point." *Lynn scores!*

We hauled two chairs and a coffee table back up to our room. It looked pretty cozy and inviting, almost like a home. But the one, big ugly desk reminded one of the work that we were there to do.

"We gotta do something about that desk," Carla announced. I don't know why I thought she'd let it go untransformed. She pulled a few things out of one of her bags, and in short order, we had a lovely dressing table with a lavender runner, candles, and a two-sided vanity mirror.

While Carla sprayed and then put her clothes carefully away in the closet and her chest of drawers, I was busy trying to figure out where she had gotten the tools and the wherewithal to paint herself this prissy shade of pink. On one hand, she displayed this crazy, bad-ass attitude, but on the other hand, she was putting some pretty nice lingerie in the drawers. I didn't see any bras or anything cotton. Sooo…Carla wanted to dress pretty underneath and live pretty in private, but in full view she seemed to want to be tough as nails. What was that all about?

With nothing else to do, I stretched out on my bunk and watched Miss Jones over my toes through the gap between the bunks.

Someone knocked on the door.

"Are you expecting anybody?" Carla asked.

"No."

Carla proceeded to plug in her radio, which sat on top of her dresser, and started trying to tune to a station. She yanked the antenna back and forth a few times.

There was another knock on the door. Annoyed, Carla walked over and opened it.

"Yes?" she said to the petite, brown-skinned woman with braids who was standing there, her arms loaded with books and papers and things.

"Hi...Carla? Lynn?"

"Yes?" Carla repeated without clarifying which one of us she was.

"I'm Janice, one of the Program Assistants. You'll meet the three other PA's later, during the week. Anyway, you guys missed the orientation session on Friday, so I'm here to kind of brief you before we get started tomorrow.

"Hey—this is nice!" Janice exclaimed as she stepped into the room, past Carla who had yet to invite her in, and surveyed our boudoir. "Where did you get all this stuff? Or was it here already when you got here?" she asked.

"Please. Come in. Have a seat," Carla said, speaking in monotone, her dry, clipped speech juxtaposed to the accompanying graceful motion of bowing and sweeping her left arm out to welcome and direct our guest.

Janice did not repeat her unanswered questions as she deposited her stack of papers on the coffee table and sat in one of the lounge chairs. I got up from my bunk and introduced myself before I switched on the reading lamp and curled up in the other lounge chair. The chairs faced each other across from the bunks, and the desk was behind Janice's chair. Carla sat at the desk. She had moved the radio from the dresser and was still tuning.

For a while Janice tried to glance Carla's way as she spoke in an attempt to include her, but it was getting uncomfortable. By the time she finished going over the program's policies, giving directions to the Blossom Cafeteria where everyone was at lunch, and reviewing the weekly schedule of courses, Janice was speaking only to me. Carla didn't seem to care. She was swaying in her seat and humming softly along with a tune on the radio. Then Janice handed us each a travel reimbursement form. Carla took an interest in this, and began to fill it out.

"I rode with Carla," I admitted, "so I didn't spend any money to be reimbursed."

"Hrumph," said Carla, reminded and obviously still sore about my lack of funds.

"That's okay. They reimburse everybody no matter what, so you still need to complete one of these."

"What?!" Carla exclaimed, whipping her body around in the desk chair to face us. I shrugged and gave her another one of my "I don't know" looks.

"How much money should I fill in then?" I asked Janice.

Carla: "The same thing I filled in—$50."

"Or you could put in the cost of whatever public transportation you would have taken," Janice suggested. "What would the bus or train have cost?"

"I have no idea."

"That would be at least $200," Carla said. I wrote $200 on the form and handed it back to Janice. "And then you can reimburse me for your trip—half," Carla continued.

"Half of what?"

"Half of what you're *getting* since that's what you *would* have paid except *I* was the one who *got* you here," Carla snapped through clenched teeth.

"That's not right! I'll give you half of $50, but if the program is giving it back to you, I don't see why you gotta have my money, too," I told her in an uncharacteristically bold move. (It must have been that thing about Taureans and money.)

"Oh, no?" Carla slammed her ink pen down, and I jumped at the sound.

Okay, I jumped at the motion.

All right—*she* scared me!

"Ah, can we wrap this up?" Janice was ready to go before she had to cut through any more tension to get out of the room. She handed us notebooks, pens, pencils, calculators, and food coupons for the week.

"You can get as much food as you want up to the value of each coupon for each meal, but if you go over that amount, then you'll have to pay the difference yourself. No using the next day's coupon.

"Well, see you tomorrow, bright and early. Remember, the MCAT starts at 8:00, so don't take too long for breakfast."

CHAPTER 13

I called Nnarami collect from the pay phone in the lobby before we left the dorm. I didn't have much to tell him—I'd slept all the way there, and hadn't done anything yet. I promised again to write.

That first day we took the MCAT, and the next two days we had pre-tests in each of our five other courses: Biochemistry, Microbiology, Physics, Statistics, and Advanced Reading. The rest of that first week, we delved right into our lectures and studying. Each class met every day, and everyone was expected to attend; there were no excused absences. We'd have three classes after breakfast, then lunch, three classes and dinner. Most of the other participants had already taken these courses because they had already graduated from college or were juniors or seniors in pre-med programs. For them, this was a review. I hadn't had these classes yet, having taken all of my electives first, so it was difficult for me to keep up. But I was determined to excel that summer. I had to show my parents that I could do something.

Carla and I ended up sitting next to each other in lectures. On the first day of pre-testing, I thought for sure she'd look to sit with her friend, Michelle, and she did. She found Michelle flanked on both sides by her roommate and yet another girl from Howard. When Michelle didn't look as if she was excited to see Carla and didn't invite her to sit with them, Carla made her way over to me. It was at that precise moment that the professors asked us not to change seats for the rest of the summer.

We ended up eating all of our meals together as well. Carla didn't even try to find other dining companions. I think she realized it would have been pointless. She kept ending up with me!

I stood in front of my dresser mirror that third morning after a shower, wrapped in a towel, frowning and tousling new, hot curls with my fingers as soon as I wound them from the barrel of the electric curlers. Carla was scheduled in the morning, and I was scheduled to take an ID picture that afternoon, otherwise I wouldn't have bothered.

"Arrrgh!"

"What's-the-matter-you?" Carla asked, sitting at the vanity in a black kimono, unwrapping her own mane from beneath a big, black scarf. Her hair was in a "beehive," which was how I thought she intended to wear it.

"I can't get my hair to do right."

"What's wrong with it?"

"The curls won't stay."

"You're over-heating it. You just did that same piece of hair three times. It probably won't curl anymore." Then Carla unwound her hair and combed it straight down all around. I was amazed that after being all coiled up (a technique she called, appropriately, a "wrap"), that it would fall straight into that perfect style that framed her face.

"Here, let me see those," she said.

I handed Carla the curlers and lowered my head when she stepped over to my dresser. She tried a curl in the back, but it did not stay; it fell immediately.

"Nope. Not gonna curl today. Just pin it up and then pull down some bangs."

Quickly, I grabbed a pin off the dresser and handed it to her over my shoulder. When Carla didn't take it from me, I looked up and met her incredulous stare in the mirror. I put the pin back down and was reaching for the curlers again when Carla suddenly grabbed a handful of my hair, almost yanking my head backwards, and twisted it around viciously. That motion would have hurt a tender-headed person, but it felt rather good to me—like a massage. Or it would have hurt the feelings of a sensitive person, but maybe I didn't have much sense. Carla took a few pins off the dresser, and proceeded to pin my hair up in back.

"Bangs," she said when she finished, and stepped over to her own dresser.

I looked in the mirror at the hair that happened to be left hanging in front. "It looks fine." Then I turned around and tried to twist my head so that I could see some of the back of my hair in the mirror. All that twisting and turning made my towel fall off.

"What in the world...?" Carla asked, stunned.

I followed her gaze to my pubic area as I figured out what was going on down there.

"Oh yeah! Well, ah, my boyfriend—you met Nnarami—he wanted to..." I started getting dressed with a quickness!

"Are those his *initials* shaved in your pubic hair, or is he trying to tell somebody something?"

"That's what I was trying to figure out!" I laughed, remembering the precise moment when I realized that Rami's initials spelled "*NO.*"

"Well, Lynn, you're pretty brave, I'll say that. Or you must really like him a lot." Carla's voice—not clipped and hard this time—lilted when she spoke. The tones went up and down for emphasis at just the right places, like she meant every word she said. Her voice had a hypnotic effect.

"I love him."

"Okay, so you love him. Does he love you, too?"

"Yeah, he does."

"How do you know?"

"Um...he likes spending time with me and taking care of me."

"Do you miss him yet?"

"Yeah, of course I do."

"Hmm. You ready to go? Give me a couple of seconds," Carla said.

Then Carla slipped off her kimono to get dressed. She wore a pretty pink and flowered camisole with matching silky boxer-like shorts. Over that, she quickly pulled on a pair of black and red nylon jogging pants and a matching jacket.

"That's cool how you wear pretty undies under regular clothes. You ever wear regular underwear?"

"Thanks. Naaah. I need space."

"Space for what?"

"For this big dick I got," she said, using her "tough" voice and grabbing her crotch. I was shocked! And intrigued. I decided I had to get some sexy lingerie for everyday use. And maybe some balls, too. Big ones.

I noticed when she went over to the desk to get her notebook that Carla was walking funny. Her arms and legs were going, but she did not move her head or her torso.

"Uh...why are you walking like that?"

"Gotta keep my head still, so I don't mess up my hair before the picture."

And she managed to keep her head still all the way over a river and through the woods to the Blossom cafeteria, all through breakfast, until her photograph was taken.

Walking through the woods on the way back to our room from Blossom one day, I started whistling *"Misty:"*

Look at me
I'm as helpless as a kitten
Up a tree

Carla suddenly broke into song as well. At first I wanted to be pissed that she would butt in and take over. On second listen, I realized she was whistling a completely different tune...

Never knowing my right foot from my left
      (Yankee Doodle came to town)

My hat from my glove
      (Riding on a pony)

I'm too misty, and too much in love
      (Stuck a feather in his cap and called it macaroni!)

We struggled to finish the songs—you can't whistle and laugh at the same time! Who knew that such opposites could be perfectly in sync and in harmony?

CHAPTER 14

Early the second week, Carla decided we would eat lunch outside the cafeteria on a picturesque veranda with lots of plants, flowers, and a picnic table. No one ever seemed to be there, so we settled down and put our lunch items on the table, side by side, and stacked the trays at the end of the table.

Somebody was approaching. I had noticed him before. He had a "mama's boy" way about him that was different from the other guys in the program. You just knew he was from down south somewhere (he was from South Carolina). He had advanced acne, a curl, and was waaaay underweight. And he did everything annoyingly slow.

"May I sit with y'all?" he asked very politely.

"Sure!" Carla said, a little friendly for her. It took me, what? a couple of *days* to get a friendly notion out of her. "Who be you?" she said, adopting some dramatic southern belle vernacular. Okay—now think of Halle Berry in *Queen*.

"I'm Leroy."

"Carla. I'm very pleased to meet you, Leroy."

I nodded at Leroy and said my name with a smile while I wondered why Carla was being nice to him. In seconds he accomplished what had taken me an entire week. He sat his tray down opposite us, braced his slight frame on the table, and threw one leg after another over the picnic bench and joined us.

"So, what brings you out here?" Carla inquired.

"I'm just tired of being around my roommate, and I didn't want to sit by myself. I saw y'all come outside. I didn't know about this table out here, but I figured there at least was some room on the ground where I could sit and eat with you."

"You're not getting along with your roomie already?" I asked.

"No, he's okay," Leroy said, then dropped his voice to a whisper. "He's just a little stinky," he confessed, scrunching up his nose for effect. Carla and I scrunched up our noses at the news.

"Eeeuuw!" Carla said. "Why is he stinky?" she whispered back conspiratorially with one hand over her mouth and nose. Carla suggested we use the "belly button test" on him. You stick your finger in a person's belly button and then smell it. If it's clean, then they probably take good care of the rest of themselves, too. If not, you should steer clear of them.

"He hasn't taken a shower yet since we got here, and he's...did you notice he's been wearing the same clothes for the past three days?"

We decided that Leroy's roommate was far beyond the belly button test.

So that's why Leroy started hanging with us, practically living with us—in order to keep away from his roommate. Even their room was all stinked up. Leroy stayed awake most nights with a headache because of the smell. One morning at breakfast he had dark circles under his eyes so bad that he looked like a malnourished woodland animal. We took one look and started calling him "Coon," which he never took offense to, considering both his name and his new nickname were synonymous with "nigger."

CHAPTER 15

I called Luke one day from a pay phone in Blossom. I thought it wouldn't hurt for him to know where I was, and I missed my brother. I gave him my address, but the only mail I got that summer was two letters from A.J. and a check from my mother, which I promptly forwarded to Howard to pay down my tuition bill. That stamped envelope set me back a whopping 34 cents!

Carla, Coon and I made flashcards out of napkins, drawing molecular structures on one side, and writing the name of the compound on the other. During study sessions, we'd play the radio really loud. Taking turns, we'd show each other the drawings. When one of us correctly named the compound, we'd toss the napkin in the air and do a little happy dance!

Against program policy, Carla got a waitressing job at a club in town. She'd work on Wednesday and Saturday nights. After her second week, Kareem, a guy who worked with her, started coming to visit. Every time he visited, I (growled at him) made a point of leaving the room and I'd get locked out because they would leave before I returned and either my key was left inside or Carla would have it (borrowed for when she went jogging, it being *only one* key). I did not like Kareem. If he wasn't around, I rationalized, Carla wouldn't leave and cause me to be locked out of my *space* and away from my *stuff*.

Soon, however, Carla decided that not only did the program not take care of all her needs, but the moonlighting didn't do it, either. She started offering massages to the guys in the program—$10 for twenty minutes. She did pretty well for a

73

while, even allowing me to get in on the business. Just when she got it into her head that she could make even more money by pimping me, the business went bust. Well, actually, she closed up shop when a guy tried to put his hands on her. All I know is that she came into the room and calmly and quietly stated, "I might have to kill Roderick." She'd slapped him, she explained, and maybe he might want to retaliate, so she would probably have to kill him first.

I was surprised that Roderick was allowed to be a customer in the first place. He blinked a lot, and only crazy people blink that much, Carla told me. I slept through most of the summer, so Carla didn't get much of a chance to check me out.

There was a bug in our room.

Luther Vandross was on the radio one night while we were relaxing, and this lightning bug was blinking in time to the music. Carla held up her hand, and he came to her and lit there for a while. Carla fell in love with that bug and named him Cody.

A few days later, we were chilling again with just the desk and reading lamps on, Carla at the desk and me on my bunk, scratching my neck. I kept feeling a tickle there, then one by my ear...

CODY!

Carla saw me looking at my hand in horror and came over to me. I was examining the carcass under the reading lamp.

"What was he doing over here, anyway? He was flying in my ear."

"You killed Cody."

"It was an accident."

"You killed my bug. You killed Cody."

"Forgive me." I stifled a giggle.

"It's not funny! You KILLED him!"

She wasn't going to let it drop that easily.

"I can fix him."

"Can you bring him back?"

"No, but I can put him back together, embalm him, and we could have a funeral." I wanted to laugh, but saw that I truly should not.

"Fix him, then."

"I need some alcohol. And toothpicks."

I laid Cody on a napkin while Carla got the alcohol and actually found a couple of toothpicks somewhere. I fixed Cody, but it wasn't good enough for Carla. She looked at my finished work, took the napkin, walked to the bathroom and flushed her pet.

"I can't have nothing in this world without somebody coming along and robbing my joy," she said.

For the next couple of days Carla terrorized me. She didn't speak. She just growled and snatched at me from her bunk as I sat studying on mine. I couldn't wait for her to get over it.

"Joseph!" Carla had taken to calling me by my last name, as our professors did in class. "You...(blah blah blah)...mattress?"

I was reading, not really paying attention, so I didn't understand what she said about a mattress. "No."

Carla left the door open and went down the hall. She was talking to Michelle.

"Oh! The mattress, huh?" I heard Michelle say, and they laughed. Then I heard Carla coming back down the hall, but she stopped in the bathroom first.

"What was that all about? You spraying mattresses for somebody?" I asked when she returned. Or maybe "mattress" was her euphemism for a sanitary napkin or something.

"Not *mattress*, MATCHES!" she laughed. "For the *match trick*."

"What is the match trick?"

"You don't know?"

I shook my head.

"Every girl needs to know about the match trick! It's for odors. Always take some matches in the bathroom with you when you gotta do number two. As *soon* as you start to let something out, strike a match, wait a few seconds, then blow it out and drop it in the toilet. Something about the sulfur…it either neutralizes the odor, absorbs it, or masks it. Anyway, keep striking matches until you flush."

"So your shit doesn't stink?"

"Riiiight!"

"Joe…Joseph…!" Carla wailed one night as she wrapped her hair.

"What's wrong?"

"My hair hurts."

"Your head?"

"No, my *hair*."

"How's you hair gonna hurt?"

"It's growing. I can feel it."

"Aw, *man*. Okay, tell me how you can *feel* your hair growing."

"I've got hair like a horse—really coarse and heavy," she explained. I got off my bunk and stepped over to the desk for a closer look.

"Nooo!" I protested.

"It's beautimous, but I'm not kidding—it'll cut ya!"

"*Beautimous*?" I laughed at the word she'd coined. Beautiful plus enormous? Full of beauty? "Let me see."

I stuck my hand underneath a mass of her hair, and—

"Ee-yah! That must hurt coming out!"

"I told you."

That weekend, we drove into town to go to a beauty shop so that Carla could get a touch-up. Don, a PA who was sweet on Carla, financed the trip—enough so that I could get my hair done, too.

Carla eyed the stylists and decided on a male one. "Male stylists are usually the best, especially if they're gay," she told me.

"Do you know how to do a wrap?" she asked a gay-looking stylist.

"A wrap? Is that like when you—"

"You wrap the hair around and sit under the dryer."

"Oh, yes, honey! We do that!"

But after he permed and washed her hair and had her in the chair, Carla realized the guy knew nothing about what he was doing. She tried to explain it to him, but he proceeded to do something else, saying, "This *is* a wrap. What kind of wrap *you* talking about?"

Carla, with her wet hair, immediately got up out of his chair, took the apron off, and went to the front counter to settle her bill for whatever he had already done.

I was impressed, because I would have just sat there and been unhappy with whatever mess the stylist made with my hair.

Anyway, I got mine cut. Off.

I missed Nnarami terribly, so I talked about him a lot.

"Are you fiending?" Carla asked.

I had to think for a second. Wordsmith that I am, I knew that "fiend" wasn't normally used as a verb, but such usage actually made perfect sense:

fiend (feend) v. to crave, be obsessed with, or addicted to something with an intensity characteristic of one who is a fiend for that thing.

(Later that fall, some singing group got a hold of Carla's word and put out a song called *"Feenin'"* in which they obviously got the word all wrong. I was annoyed every time I heard someone say "feenin'" for about a year after that.)

Anyway, yes, I was *fiending*, I confessed.

"Whenever I was 'bad,' he'd say, 'Your horns are showing,' and so I'd show them to him, like this," I said, pointing my index fingers up from the sides of my head.

"Whenever he was bad, though, he was *sooo* bad that he had to use both his arms."

Carla said, "Like this?" and did it exactly the way Rami did—she even had the same silly grin on her face so that she looked a lot like him!

I asked her to do it over and over again for me, and she always would.

Since I was fiending, I tried to get as close as possible to someone who was as close as possible to Rami—in this case, another Alpha in the program named Brian. Brian and I had this "Let's pretend we're married" game going on that he would have won if Carla hadn't kept him at bay by growling at him, and if she hadn't literally dragged me out of some uncompromising situations.

I talked to Luke one other time that summer. I said something stupid and he growled at me!

"What did you just say?" Carla was standing next to me at the payphone in Blossom, so I held the receiver out to her so she could hear him growl at me again. Her eyes got wide, and then she covered her mouth with both hands and giggled!

All funning aside, Luke had some news for me.

"Lynn, I really hate to do this, but I gotta tell you something. Everybody thought it would be best if you heard it from me."

He took a deep breath, blew it out, and began.

"Kevin McDonald—

—got married last week.

And his new wife?

She's only 19."

It was a good thing Carla was in the room with me when *"Congratulations"* by Vesta Williams came on the radio that evening. She squeezed into a lounge chair with me and held me, rocking, while I tried to sing and cry at the same time:

> *Congratulations…I thought it would have been me*
> *(Standing there with you)*
> *Congratulations…I hope you're happy*
> *'Cause as long as I can breathe*
> *You'll always be the one for me.*

"There, now," Carla crooned. "You know what? I never met a Kevin that I liked. Something about that name…they're all crazy."

The next bug we encountered in our room was no laughing matter for either one of us. We heard him before we saw him. He was so big that he actually made noise as he crawled along the radiator:

> *tiptiptiptiptiptiptiptiptiptiptiptiptiptip!*

"It's…a BIG BUG!" Carla yelled when she finally got a look at him. She jumped down from her bunk, ran over to her closet, pulled out her suitcase and started packing.
"I'm going back to Baltimore!"
"Carla, don't go. It's just a bug!"
"It's a BIG bug. Either HE goes, or *I* go."
"Okay, okay…"

"Kill him, Joe." (Carla had gotten tired of saying "Joseph," and just shortened it to Joe.)

"I can't! Let me go get somebody."

I was not about to step on that big bug and have him all mushed up under my foot. Plus, I was still a little gun-shy about the whole Cody incident.

A girl from across the hall came over and wrangled him for us so that no one had to leave.

Normally, I would fail physics. "I have a mental block," is how I'd explain having failed it both in high school and in college. But either I took it enough times so that something finally stuck, or I just got over it, because I was doing great and other "Success" (SC-SSS) participants started coming to me for help! I received a letter from A.J. addressed to *Lynn "Phyz Wiz" Joseph.* I hadn't called or written him back, but I never stopped to wonder how he knew.

As for the rest of my classes...I was doing okay in statistics, but not great enough to stand out. Biology was interesting, but no cigar. And if I once thought *physics* was hard, then biochemistry was likely to *kill* me, even with the flashcard study sessions! And all we did in our MCAT preparation course was take parts of old practice tests.

One day on the way to the Advanced Reading lab, I overheard another participant talking excitedly about his performance in that class, one that nobody seemed to be taking seriously. His interest in that class and his excitement were infectious. I hadn't given reading much thought because it was just one of those things that I did naturally (and did well). But then it occurred to me that 1) *I* was in control of how well I did in that class, 2) it was the only subject that I had some solid background in, and 3) I really enjoyed it. I decided that Advanced Reading was where I would make my mark!

Dr. Proctor was a Dean who gave a fascinating and informative seminar on interviewing techniques. This was no ordinary information, however. He showed us subtle ways to intimidate the interviewer ("Try not moving your head *at all*"). Carla was thrilled to learn she already possessed a talent that increased her intimidation factor and enabled her never to be jobless again! He also showed us how to play a vicious game called "Spoons," which left us battered and bruised, but taught us a lot about competition. We finished early, so he sat and talked with us, instructing us on how we could attend every single party during med school and still make the grades. Dr. Proctor was waaay cool.

Carla decided that she, Coon and I should take him out to lunch, and he accepted our invitation. I was charged with the simple task of making the reservations.

"We don't take reservations," the restaurant lady told me.

"Did you make the reservations?" Carla asked when I returned to our room.

"No. They said they don't take reservations."

"Come with me," she said.

I followed Carla back to the phone in the lobby and dialed the restaurant's number for her.

"I am making reservations for lunch for four this Saturday at 12:30 pm. The name is Jones. Thank you." And she hung up.

When we got to the place on Saturday, she walked in past some people waiting and said, "Reservations for Jones, party of four for lunch." We were seated promptly.

At lunch, Dr. Proctor dropped all manner of science on us ("The quest in life is to see clearly what is in front of your eyes" and "Europe ruled, but Africa reigned"). He was deep—too deep for me and Coon, but Carla thoroughly enjoyed herself. Coon and I were just in awe of the crazy/cool man who told us how to have fun and allowed us to damn near kill each other in his seminar. Then Dr. Proctor recited a poem, delivered so dramatically that we were spellbound until it ended with the advice that sometimes you need to tell somebody, "Yo mama!" I think it must have been an original poem.

When Don the PA (who paid for our hair) had all the Success participants over to his condo for a pool party, it became evident to everyone (including me) that Carla knew her way around his place. Carla explained that while she liked Don *("He's 'belly-plenty!'")*, she just really needed to luxuriate in a bathtub.

One participant had a real crush on Don, so she had an attitude with Carla *and* me for the rest of the summer. She was funky "den a mongfecky," Carla said, in her best imitation of her 4-year-old neighbor-boy saying, "...than a motherfucker!"

Michelle Wilson was "smug den a mongfecky." We dubbed other Success participants:

> fashion
> acidosis
> drunk
> monster
> genius
> freak
> Dance Fever
> hibiscus
> Charles
> married
> M.I.A.
> and bad... den a mongfecky!

I used to be "phat den a mongfecky" until I made the mistake of sharing our list with the person sitting to my right in class. Then Carla called me "social." (Shit.)

Carla's favorite mode of expression was the ode, and she wrote lots of them. "An Ode to My Captain" was about a snooty Success participant who had an entourage ("She 'O Captain, My Captain' den a mongfecky!"). "An Ode to Pimping" served as a warning to me, after she caught Brian in our room. "An Ode to Boots" was notification that she had borrowed a pair of mine, and later, her crowning achievement…"An Ode to Odes":

> *"When you're in a shitty mode,*
> *Sit right down and write an ode!*
> *An ode to this, an ode to that*
> *An ode to my dick or my booty phat!*
> *An ode to love, an ode to hate*
> *An ode to Bob Marley, the one I just ate*
> *An ode to the person down the hall*
> *An ode to the critics—fuck them all!*
> *An ode to the child, an ode to the fool*
> *An ode to the poet (me)—Damn. I'm cool.*
> *An ode to the dumb cow/slutting pig-assed fool/*
> *   mutha-fucking bitch*
> *And to whatever else rhymes with it!*
> *Are you in a shitty mode?*
> *Turn it out and write an ode!"*

Odes made Carla feel better about things—and you'd feel better, too, unless you were the subject or cause of her writing one.

We took to hanging out in the basement lounge, usually after we finished working out on the stationary bikes. Toward the end of summer, the other Success participants discovered our little spot and started to hang down there, too. We even started to play together…those silly get-naked exploitation games like "Sleepers" and "Judge & Jury." I'm surprised there are people who still don't know about them.

We were nearing the end of our eight weeks when one of the professors invited Carla to dinner at his place. She thought he might try to kiss her, so she talked him into making it a cookout at his place for all the Success participants.

Success was every bit as hard as it had promised it would be. I did fine though, earning a couple of A's, a couple of B's, one C, and fair-to-middling scores on the practice MCAT.

There was a nice banquet on the last day. Carla's mother and brother came from Baltimore, and my cousin Larry and his family (whom I had never in life laid eyes on) were in attendance as well, stopping through on their way to Columbus, Georgia. I had talked to my grandmother (my *real* grandmother, Nettie, in Gary) and she hooked that up.

I did it! I was supposed to win an award for having the fastest reading rate (1473 words per minute). I could just picture showing it to my mother! But as I waited for them to say, *"This year's Highest Reading Rate Award goes to Young Dr. Lynn Joseph,"* they announced that this year, they'd decided to give it to the participant with the *most improved* rate. Now, *that* pissed me off because the guy really wasn't "most improved." He didn't know that the pre-test was timed, so he didn't finish it. Therefore, he couldn't do anything *but* "improve" on the post-test.

And finally…after eight weeks…after splurging a nickel or a dime at a time at Blossom and purchasing some toothpaste, I still had $1.00 left!

CHAPTER 16

On July 31, we returned to Washington, D.C. I was not at all refreshed, but I was raring to go. Surely nothing could possibly be as challenging as Success!

Carla was going to just drop me off at Luke's place, but when they simultaneously growled at each other in greeting, she decided to stay and visit for a while. So Carla parked the car legally and helped me carry my two bags upstairs to the apartment.

"How long do you plan on staying?" Luke asked, first thing. I lit into my brother right away.

"What? You don't want me to stay here?"

"I didn't—"

"And another thing—if you were tired of me staying with you, why didn't you just say something?"

"Who said I was tired of you?"

"Your mother and your father!"

"Aw, man, naw! Don't listen to them. You know you my baby," Luke crooned, grabbing my head in the crook of his arm and licking the side of my face.

"Euuuuww!" Carla laughed. I struggled to get away from Luke, and Carla ran across the room to help. We managed to tumble to the hardwood floor, landing in a big heap with Luke on the bottom with his shirt pushed up to his chest. I held him down while Carla tickled him, and later I found out that that's when she made her move on his belly button.

The phone rang, and since I was closest to it, I answered.

"Hello?"

"Hello?" said a woman's voice. It sounded like my mother. "I think I must have the wrong number."

"Oh. Okay," I said, and hung up the phone. Was that my mother?

The phone rang again. I picked it up.

"Hello?"

"Sorry, I have the wrong—"

"Ma? It's me, Lynn."

"Oh..." She sounded a little unsure, like she might have thought I didn't want to talk to her, so I tried to sound upbeat.

"We just got back from South Carolina, me and my roommate, Carla. We're in here picking on Luke." I looked over at them, still tussling on the floor, and laughed.

"That's nice," she said hesitantly. "How was it?"

"It was hard because I hadn't had most of those classes before, like everybody else. I think I was the youngest person there! Anyway, I did pretty good. Got a couple of A's, a couple of B's, a C, did okay on the MCAT, oh! and I had the fastest reading rate of anybody in the program!"

"Oh, good...good."

"Hey, ma? Thanks for the money. I sent it to Howard along with the money I was reimbursed from the program, so now I can get registered."

"So you're going back to Howard?"

"I'll still be going to both schools."

"Oh. You going to be staying there with your brother?"

"For a little while, until I get a job so I can pay for my own place." Shit! I realized I wasn't saying anything new! My underarms were tingling. It was time to get off the phone. "So, you want to talk to Luke?"

I decided I'd better get started making things happen quickly. The next day, Tuesday, August 1, I called Frank. Frank was my ex-boss at La Vie, a quaint little bistro and grocery store where I had worked my sophomore year. So when Irene and Sheila called me asking if I'd like to share a house with them, with the prospect of getting my old job back I told them that I surely would! They found a rowhouse (get it? "Rho" house) on 3rd Street for the three of us and one other tenant.

CHAPTER 17

We were slated to move in by August 15, but had to have the lease signed and first month's rent and a security deposit by the week before. Sheila and Irene agreed to this date against my wishes, as I had already informed them that even without a pay lag from my new job, I wouldn't have the money—$450—until the 18th. They were more worried about the fourth girl showing up.

That Tuesday, we met on the front steps of the house— me with A.J., and Irene and Sheila. The landlord was inside fixing up. We were supposed to sign the lease and pay that day, or else risk losing the house to some other prospective renters.

"What do we do if Christie doesn't get here before Mr. Smith leaves?" Irene wondered.

"What time is it? And when's he leaving?" A.J. asked.

"Probably soon. It's already 1:30," Sheila said. "We're real short unless we can figure something out by 4:00 or so. Not only don't we have enough people, but now we're definitely not going to have all the money. I mean, I think Irene and I can cover Lynn, but not Christie, too."

"How much is rent?" A.J. asked.

"Twelve hundred a month, three hundred each."

"Plus we need six hundred for the security deposit," Irene explained. "That's one hundred fifty each."

"All right...tell you what. I'm here, I'll be the fourth roommate. And I've even got a check from my dad that was for *my* new place, but oh well. So now Lynn's covered, right?"

Sheila and Irene were delighted. A.J.'s check needed to be cashed, though, because Mr. Smith wasn't going to be the third party to a personal check. We all decided to walk downtown to Irene's bank. A.J. signed it over to her to cash, and she needed to get her money out.

So we walked thirty minutes to the bank, but because Irene took so much of her money out, there weren't any funds against which to cash A.J.'s check.

"Lynn, we really need your money, and we need it now," Irene said in a frustrated tone.

"Where do you think I can get four hundred and fifty dollars in an hour?"

Silence, and then...

"Get an advance on your paycheck."

They knew that I was cool with my boss and that I had been able to do that times before. I was peeved that they would ask me to take advantage of Frank's and my relationship that way; I had only been back on the job for a week! They didn't care, though. The money was due, or nobody was moving in.

My armpits got hot and tingly. I needed to *do* something to get the sweat to actually start flowing, or it would needle me to death. I turned on my heel and struck out walking to my job on the other side of town, at least five miles away. A.J. struck out with me. He didn't say a word, just made sure that when I went stepping off curbs without looking, that there were no cars in my way!

Frank was a little miffed about the advance, but he let me have it anyway. And he offered A.J. a job, too!

A.J. convinced me that I wasn't punishing Irene and Sheila by walking, so I agreed to take a cab (which he paid for) back to the house. We gave Mr. Smith the signed lease, handed over our money, and he handed us a copy of the keys. It was two days before move-in.

A.J. went off to break the news to his ex-new housemates, and Irene, Sheila, and I were walking from the house back to campus when I spied a rather clean white van driving by. The driver kept looking our way, so I waved to him. He pulled over abruptly at the next corner and stopped. I walked over.

"I was just admiring your clean white van," I said.

"You like it, huh?" asked the driver. He was an older man, I guessed, from the gray in his hair and full beard, but not too much older. At just 20, though, most people seemed "older" to me.

"Yeah. I could use a van like this," I said, getting close enough to peer inside his window, which was rolled all the way down. He was resting his arm on it, the other hand hanging coolly by the wrist over the steering wheel. The van was clean as a whistle in the back, too, as far as I could tell in the dark.

"What do you need a van for?" he asked. He really was good-looking, with smooth, Hershey bar colored skin, pretty lips from what I could see of them, and perfectly perfect white teeth. He was suitable for kissing, but I wasn't thinking about that.

"We're moving into a house around the corner from here, but none of us has a car. You want to move us?"

"That's what I do," he said, reaching for a business card on the dash. He handed it to me. Sullivan Moving and Storage.

"Oh," I said, taking the card and waiting for him to give me an estimate. He gave me an estimate, all right!

"What's your name?" he asked.

"Lynn. What's yours? Are you Michael?" I asked, reading the card.

"Mike. Pleased to meet you." We shook hands through the window. "So when would you like to move?"

"By Monday. But we don't have any money."

"I haven't asked you for any."

"Yeah, but you're a real business and everything..."

"We'll work it out. How much stuff do you have?" I tell you, people sure were fixated on how much stuff I had!

"Not much," I said, thinking of my two or three duffel bags and a few boxes of books and memorabilia. I didn't have any furniture at my brother's place. I forgot to consider that Sheila and Irene had furnished apartments, and I also forgot to mention that we weren't all three of us moving from the same place.

Somehow Sheila got Mike and his partner to move her things first that weekend. She had an entertainment center and a big, heavy sofabed that nearly broke Mike's back. He'd be okay, though. He was just 36, we learned. I was all set to go next, but Irene insisted that she had to be out of her place the next day or else. So the next day, they moved Irene. She had a sofabed, too, and a dining room set as well. Mike was a little undone by then. He was talking about quitting this job for which he was not getting paid. I had to call him the next day.

"You coming?"

"I don't know, man, my back is killing me."

"Please, Mike, come on."

"How much stuff you got, really?"

"I swear I only have, like, three bags and four boxes. And a trunk. It's a little one, though. It'll just take one trip, and I only live about fifteen minutes from the house. Please?" I could not BELIEVE I might not get my stuff moved when I was the one who found Mike in the first place.

Mike could not resist. He met me at my brother's apartment without his assistant and quickly loaded up my few boxes and bags. And trunk.

"Get in for a minute," he said to me from the back of the van. I looked at him quizzically for a second. He was parked right in front of the apartment house. He couldn't be thinking... I started walking around to the passenger side of the van.

"No, back here," he said.

I walked to the back and climbed in. Mike closed the doors. All my stuff was stacked neatly near the front of the van. There was a tire laying by the back doors with a stack of folded blankets on top. He had used these when he moved Sheila's and Irene's furniture, to keep it from getting scratched. Now he was lying back against them and the tire.

"What?" I asked.

"Come here."

I scooted within arm's reach of him, and he did just that—reached for my arms and pulled me down on top of him. Our faces were centimeters apart.

"How old are you again?" he asked.

"Twenty. Why?" He really was attractive, but I was uncomfortable with his choice of settings.

"Just...nothing," he said. Then he kissed me. I had never kissed anybody with a full beard and mustache before. I had never kissed a *grown man* before. It wasn't anything different. He was a good kisser, you know, not wet and sloppy, not groping me or anything. It was new, so it should have been exciting, but I was thinking about Nnarami. I wondered when he'd be back. I wondered if this would be considered cheating or not. Surely it was. After only thirty seconds or so, I couldn't stand the guilt. I moved my hands to Mike's chest to push him away, but was totally taken aback when my bra came undone and Mike's hands weren't even under my T-shirt. Just one quick little squeeze and that was it! I was impressed with his skill, but I guess he *should* have been good at it because of course he'd been unhooking bras from *waaay* back.

Mike gave my left breastlet his undivided attention. I call them "breastlets" because they're so small. I've heard that more than a handful is a waste (I kept meaning to ask Irene about that), but a handful is about all I've got. Mike seemed to be okay with that, though. I was just kind of kneeling there in front of him, looking down at the top of his head, noting that he was going bald and knowing that this definitely had to be considered cheating.

"Mike, stop."

"What's wrong?"

"Nothing. I just don't want to...you know...here," I said, hooking my bra back and straightening my T-shirt.

Mike didn't say a word. I hoped I hadn't hurt his feelings. I still had to get my stuff across town! He opened the doors and helped me out of the back of the van, seeming unperturbed enough. He smiled, anyway, and let me get into the front seat of the van for the ride to my house. I relaxed. We chatted easily during the fifteen-minute ride, and as he unloaded my things. Then it was time for him to go. There was no more work for him to do for free.

"When can I see you again?" he asked as he started the ignition.

Arrgh. I thought about Nnarami again. When was he coming home?

"We're having a party on Labor Day. Around 3:00. Why don't you, uh, stop by?" I told him. I didn't think he would want to be bothered with a bunch of college kids. Even if he did, it was safe, I thought. He couldn't molest me at a party.

"Stop by," he repeated.

"Yeah, stop by."

"On Labor Day."

"On Labor Day," I confirmed.

"All right," he said, giving me a peck on the lips (ummmm?...*naaaah!*) and turning to get into the van.

"And if you can't make it then," I added, since I didn't really mean to issue the invitation in the first place (Nnarami might be there!), "you know where we are!" Anyway, I didn't think Mike would enjoy our teenybopper party. He gave me a bland smile, a weak wave, and drove away. I watched him leave, then went in the house to unpack and clean up.

Sheila got the huge room with the big bay window on the front of the house. Irene got the huge room with a glass-enclosed sun porch on the back of the house. A.J. and I had identical cells next to each other along the hallway. Since Sheila and Irene had such large rooms and didn't want to pay more rent for them, they agreed to pay all the utilities. Later on they'd find out how much it cost to heat a three-story row house.

The house was not far from campus—within walking distance—but just far enough that people would think twice about "dropping by" for a visit. This also made us think twice about going to class, though, and subsequently, we all missed a lot of school that year. This turned out to be the first one of a couple or even a *few* senior years for each of us: *first* senior, *second* senior, *super* senior, and then answering that nagging question:

"When are you graduating?"

with a non-specific:

"In May."

I tried to make my own private cell livable. Hattie loaned me a fold-up, roll-away cot. It squeaked and rolled every time I *looked* at it, but at least I had somewhere to lay my head. I promptly sprayed the mattress, then added my "desert sun and sand dunes" ensemble, which made the cot look deceptively more stable and comfortable than it really was.

I "picked up" a few crates from behind a McDonald's, borrowed another one from A.J., and stacked them on their sides by twos. Mini bookcases! I put my textbooks inside. A wide, sturdy piece of drywall from the basement was covered in wood grain contact paper and placed on top of the crates for a makeshift desk.

Not many of my clothes were meant for hanging in a closet, but since I had no bureau, I hung them all. I left my panties, bras, and socks in the trunk with some other odds and ends, though.

I looked around my humble little abode. It was pitiful.

Come nightfall that first full day, we became painfully aware that there were no window treatments anywhere in the house.

"Do you know how much it will cost to get blinds for all of these windows?" Irene-with-three-walls-of-glass asked.

"Yeah," Sheila-with-the-front-bay-windows agreed.

"Lynn and I only have one window to cover," noted Prisoner Cell Block A.J.

"No, I'm talking about downstairs, too. We need to all pitch in and get these windows covered."

"Like I said—do you know how much that will cost?" Irene griped.

"We can just do a little at a time," I ventured.

"Well, what do you propose we do in the meantime?" A.J. wanted to know.

"We could just tape some newspaper up or something," Irene suggested. Sheila and A.J. didn't like that idea—and said so—but didn't interfere.

"People will think we've got something in here we don't want them to see," Sheila explained.

"They saw everything there was to see when we moved it in. And tonight when they look in, they'll see they were right— ain't nothing in here!" I informed her.

"It'll look tacky," Sheila added.

"Not as tacky as you changing your clothes in front of your bedroom window."

"Aaaah-*ha*! I *see*. Well in *that* case, I'll start with the *Style* section," Sheila laughed, good-naturedly.

So we taped newspaper to the windows until we finished measuring and fitting them with blinds a month later.

Rumor had it that ours was once a crack house, and that someone had been killed inside! We thought we could make out the large bloodstain on the carpet just inside the front door.

"That dark spot bothers me," Sheila said. "I wonder what the floor looks like under the carpet."

"Let's pull it up and see!" I was curious. Besides, I love wood. Don't care for carpet much.

"Naaaah," Irene droned.

"Come on! Let's do it!" I begged. "Anyway, that's probably where that dog smell is coming from."

"That *pissy* dog smell."

"Yeah, let's pull it up."

It was barely twenty minutes later when we were looking at the large foyer and living room hardwood floor. It was in need of sanding and refinishing, so we put Sheila in charge of finding someone to do that before the Labor Day party.

Next, we scrutinized the dining room, which we decided to tile. At $15 per box of only nine tiles, that project had us going until Homecoming.

Luke came by to check out my new digs and to measure my room so that he and Bill could come and build me some furniture. My brothers were so smart and talented! With so little space, they decided that I needed a loft, and got right to work designing one.

As I excitedly pointed out our handiwork throughout the house, Luke became convinced that I was crazy.

"Why are you guys spending money to improve somebody else's house?"

"We gotta live in it!"

"Not for long, though."

"What do you mean? We're not going anywhere. Maybe one day we'll even buy the house!"

"Yeah, okay."

"Sure! Mr. Smith kinda said so. He likes what we've been doing. He even offered to redo the sun room with real terra cotta tiles that match the fake ones in the dining room."

"I'll bet he *does* appreciate you adding to the value of his house for him."

The last order of business, since I had secured a job, a place to live, and schedules for classes at both schools, was to pick up where I left off with Nnarami. I knew he would be back in town soon—if not for the first two days of class (Thursday and Friday before Labor Day, *du-uuh*), then certainly for the first frat meeting of the year which was scheduled for that Friday. I used the pay phone on the corner to leave our address on his answering machine.

On our first Saturday night in the house, Kern spent the night with her Alpha boyfriend, Rick. Sometime around 5:00 that morning, I was awakened by a bunch of hollering and screaming coming from downstairs where they were sleeping. Then someone was climbing in my bed! It was Buddy, number two from the Alpha line the year before.

"Get out of my bed!" I yelled. *Didn't he know I was Rami's woman? Where was Rami?*

"Ah, come on!" Buddy pleaded.

I let him have it (the bed) while I ran down the stairs to see who was making the other disturbance. I ran into Irene and Sheila on the way. A.J. had to be dead or not at home.

"That fool Buddy was trying to get in my bed! I don't like him!"

"I know," Irene said. "Derrick was trying to get in mine."

Sheila: "What is going on down there?"

There were about fifteen bro's stumbling all over our living room, all over Kern and Rick, who had been sleeping on the sofabed. Most of them had McDonald's bags, and were pulling out breakfast. I looked around carefully. Nnarami wasn't there.

"Hey! It's a housewarming!" Sheila said. "*Ho-oh!*" she sang. "*Ho-oh!*"

"*Ho-oh*! *Ho-oh*!" said everybody. And the space invaders from upstairs came down to join us, and we all ate the housewarming breakfast.

CHAPTER 18

Nnarami stopped by the house two nights later.

The first thing he said was: "You cut your hair." Where was that special smile!, the big hug, the kisses, and the release of pent-up passion? He looked yummy, but there was definitely a chill coming off of him...like ice cream.

Rami's own hair was styled in a fade with a part on the side. He'd also gained a considerable amount of weight—all muscle. His shoulders were wide before, but now they were thick, and his chest down to his waist was shaped like a "V." *Oooh.* But why was he acting so different?

"Yes, I cut my hair." I knew it was pretty ugly, too. I was locked out of the house (!) on Monday and decided to stop by the beauty shop on the corner while I waited for Irene, Sheila, or A.J. to get home. I went into the shop and made the mistake of saying, "Can you trim it for me?" and then proceeded not to pay attention. Luckily I've got that "wash and wear" kind of hair.

"Why did you cut your hair?"

"It was hot."

"I told you never to cut your hair."

"I know. It was hot," I repeated.

"But I told you not to."

I ignored him.

"How was your summer?" he asked.

"Hard. How was yours?" *Was he still not answering questions?*

"I missed you." *Yep!*

"I missed you, too."

"Why didn't you write to me?"

"Irene said you left for Jamaica."

"I would have gotten your letters."

"Oh. Well, there wasn't much to tell. It was just school."

"You could have told me what you were feeling."

I thought about that.

We sat on the front steps of the house for about fifteen minutes without touching or talking while I fiddled with my keychain. *My Man Is An Alpha.*

"About that pain you were having—"

"What pain?"

"You know…"

"Oh."

"You should see a doctor. I think you've got something called P.I.D.—Pelvic Inflammatory Disease."

"Pelvic Inflammatory Disease?"

"That's right."

"I don't think so. I had a complete physical for school, and they didn't mention anything about it."

"Get yourself checked."

"Okay, I will." *Please! Apparently, getting buffed up had made him forget he was already beefed up!*

"Well, I've got to go." Rami stood and brushed off his— jeans! I noticed he was wearing jeans. He only wore slacks before. He looked *sooo* cute in them, but hey…new body, new hair, new jeans—*new attitude.* Yes, that was it! This wasn't the guy I had fallen in love with. *That* guy would have shown me his special smile!, hugged me like there was no tomorrow, and…and…*ummm!*

This so-and-so, however, had stood up from the steps and was walking away.

"Are you coming back? To our Labor Day party?"

"I don't know. I might go to Virginia Beach." Virginia Beach was the Back-To-School "Meat Market," where all the beautiful black college kids went to ah…be seen? And hook up. *Anyway…*

"Oh."

"Do you have a phone yet?"

"No, I haven't gotten it turned on yet."

"Get a phone so that I can call you. Bye."

That Friday, Irene's mother showed up for a week's visit. She was happy to cook all the food for the party, so we had a nice Labor Day Barbecue.

Nnarami didn't come because he did go to Virginia Beach, but yes, Mike was there. He didn't seem to enjoy himself, and he didn't visit or call again after that. But Irene's mom? We looked up, and she was still there a month later. Our style was seriously cramped! She must have figured she was wearing out her welcome when we started calling her by her first name. So she went back to New Jersey...then packed her bags, and moved back to DC permanently!

Carla drove down from Baltimore to attend the barbecue. Afterwards, she asked if she could camp out at the house for a while until she got herself together to go to medical school. My housemates all adored her, recognizing the inspiration for the "big balls" I'd come back bragging about, digging the new nickname ("Joe") that she had bestowed upon me, and appreciating being taught the secret of odorless bathrooms. It was fine with them, and besides, she would be in *my* room. That was cool with me, because between working and visiting Luke (!), she really wasn't there a lot.

And she didn't have much stuff!

CHAPTER 19

I finally got a phone, and Nnarami called frequently to invite me over. Irene and Sheila would walk me to campus, Rami would meet us there, and he and I would walk to his apartment together. He still seemed a little distant, though. Irene and Sheila agreed that the "Voodoo Jeans" must have had him under a spell. He only came by the house one more time, but *woo hoo!* That was the time my housemates confirmed that my bedroom floor was directly above the dining room!

We had a booth at the annual "Back to School" day, where all the different clubs and organizations get to meet and greet the freshmen and new entrants to hand out information about their activities.

The Sigma Gamma Rho table was sparsely decorated, and most of the paraphernalia was stuff we had made on line. Compare that to the other sororities, whose tables were overflowing with stuff from stores and years, and we looked right pitiful!

Nnarami stopped by our booth for a brief moment. He looked at it, looked at another table, looked at our table again, shook his head, and then strolled over to the beckoning AKA's next to us to socialize for a while.

My sorors looked at me. I shrugged my shoulders. *"I don't know."*

Our chapter was pressed for manpower and strapped for cash, so when it was time to do anything, we all had to pitch in, even doing things like making flyers and posters by hand. Anything anyone was willing and able to do was acceptable.

I drew dancing stick figures on the flyers for our first party. They looked sort of like hieroglyphics doing the "Walk Like an Egyptian" thing. I thought they were cute. My sorors only cared that there were flyers at all to post. We supposed we'd find out later what the general public thought of them by how many people paid attention and came to the dance, but meanwhile, Rami was quite vocal about it: "That's tacky. You can do better than that."

The flyers for our first information session rated a "Getting better," from His-High-and-Mightiness, and finally, we got a nod for our "Gold Rush" posters.

But we definitely were having trouble. First, only a few people stopped by our "Back to School" booth, next to the AKA table, as it was; then the Delta's—at the last minute—threw a party the same night as ours; and finally, the three girls who came to our information session were actually lost, looking for the Zeta Rush upstairs.

Needless to say, Sigma didn't need Rami's destructive criticism, and I didn't need to be the one whose boyfriend was dishing it out.

Then Rami's calls tapered off. I stopped calling him as much, too. I decided that if I was being dissed, I would do some dissing back.

One day after this had been going on for a few weeks, Irene and I saw him on campus, later in the afternoon when our classes were over and I didn't have to go to UDC for any mortuary science classes. He seemed to be in pretty good spirits. Rami followed us all around campus trying to talk me into going to his apartment with him. I refused. I told him I didn't want to talk to him, but he kept following. I loved it! But then we ran into a bunch of bro's, and he forgot all about me.

Irene suggested we go talk to Derrick, so we walked to his dorm one night, halfway between our house and campus. I was a little uncomfortable because I hardly ever even talked to

Derrick, let alone knew him well enough to ask any favors, but I figured Irene had an ulterior motive.

Fortunately, we caught him at home. He flung open the door to his room as soon as Irene knocked and then retreated into a sea of papers and mess all over his floor.

"Excuse the mess. Come on in."

I came in last, closed the door behind me, and stood right in that spot, while Irene trampled over to his bed and made herself at home. By then, I could recognize when someone was unduly familiar with a place. I deduced that the hooking up Irene and Rami had discussed at the beginning of the summer had already taken place!

"We need you to talk to Rami," Irene told him.

"What's going on?"

I tried to answer ("He's being…he's just…") but I didn't know what to say. Derrick looked up from the mess he was trying to organize. I guess he hadn't seen me standing behind Irene when he'd opened the door. He smiled. Derrick had a really cute smile with dimples—almost like the smile I hadn't seen in a while—, which made me feel a little warm as I smiled shyly back at him. Then he waded over and gave me a big hug.

I like hugs, and I like to think I give good ones. I don't just kind of lean over the other person and tap them on the back, oh no! I give *full-body* hugs! That's where you lay your entire body on the other person, connecting in as many places as possible. Then you hold on tight for a few moments, because if you don't, somebody might lose their balance! Now *that's* a genuine hug—one that says "I'm happy to see you!"

Then you can throw in something special for members of the opposite sex, like a little back rub, or the "hook"—wrapping one of your legs around one of theirs (which puts you even MORE off balance). These hugs beg the question: "Is that a *banana* in your pocket?!"

"What's up, *sands?* I didn't see you come in."

"Do you think you can talk to Rami for me? Find out what's up with him?"

"He's acting stupid and he needs me to stick my foot up his ass, is that right?"

"Well, maybe not all that."

"Cool. I'll talk to him. He hasn't hurt you or anything, has he?"

"Oh, no! Nothing like that."

"Good," Derrick said, chucking me on the chin. Maybe I was still giving off those "little buddy" vibes. Damn.

"What's up with you, lady?" he said to Irene. They started talking, and I just took a seat at the desk and daydreamed about things working out, because Derrick was going to talk to Rami and straighten him out for me.

CHAPTER 20

Although we worked hard to promote a positive "Sigma Image" on campus, some pretty racy practices went on in our house.

"You know we're living in a brothel," Sheila announced one day.

"Why? Because we all hoes?" Irene said, laughing.

"No, seriously. Any house occupied by three or more women is considered a brothel," Sheila stated matter-of-factly. We waited for the punch line, but there was none. So we were quiet for a minute, thinking about that. It made sense, especially for our house. We'd actually spend time working out things like the "S cycle:"

> Shit,
> Shower,
> Shave,
> Shampoo,
> Seek (a date),
> Sup (eat),
> Cinema,
> Sex,
> Sex,
> Sleep.

The goal was to complete an S cycle once you started it, and if you got stuck at any one of the stages for more than 24 hours, you were just *sorry* and had to start all over.

Then there were the "three F's"—find 'em, feed 'em, and fuck 'em. We decided to split it up and make a game out of it.

Whenever a guy showed up at the house, he was considered "found." If he was ugly, the other two would rush around trying to find something for him to eat. I always kept some chips or something in my room, so that I didn't get stuck with that last part. My sorors ruled that chips didn't count, though, after I got away with it a couple of times. It had to be *real* food.

The game was especially challenging for me because I wasn't interested in getting any action; I was holding out for when Rami came to his senses. I was in dry-dock, but not desperate! Yet.

Sometimes the three F's worked out fine, and sometimes they didn't. We would be out at a party, and if one of us was interested in a guy, we had to get the other two to invite him to the house and offer him some food—*not* an easy task when your girls want to mess with you! And sometimes if you brought a fine one home, the other two would get excited, so you had to let them know that you were doing an *S cycle* and not the *three F's*—that you intended to find, feed, *and* fuck this one all by yourself!

The three B's were kick the ballistics, get the booty, and be gone, but it wasn't as popular as the other two. I think it was something we picked up from some frat boys.

Anyway, like I said, I wasn't getting in on any of this action because I was waiting around for Rami to exorcise that demon he had in him. I knew he was upset about me cutting my hair, but dog! It wasn't that bad. It was growing back already.

One Friday night, the second week of September, Irene, Sheila, and I were walking home from a party on campus when a small white car, a Dodge Omni, turned a corner really close in front of us. Then it stopped and the driver, a young man, rolled down the window and yelled to us:

"Hey! Whose car is this?"

We looked at him like he was crazy, because 1) he almost ran over us, and 2) it was obviously *his* car—he was driving it—

until we realized it was Luke. And my mother was in the car with him.

"It's your brother, Joe!"

"I see! Hey! Whose car is this?" I asked, walking over to him.

"See? I knew she would say that. Didn't I just say that?" Luke could be so corny!

"Is it Mom's? Hey, Ma! What are you doing here? Is this your new car?"

"No. It's yours," she smirked with her left eyebrow raised as she got out. That was her "I'm pretty pleased with myself" look.

"For me?" I raised my right eyebrow back at her.

A normal "surprised" look consists of two raised eyebrows, so I wasn't trying to look skeptical, or smug like my mother, but I haven't been able to raise both of my eyebrows since the 6th grade. Like hundreds of thousands of other prepubescent girls, I had read Judy Blume's *Are You There God? It's Me, Margaret.* That Margaret was cool as hell! and she only raised one eyebrow. I trained my eyebrow to do the same thing. But while my talent was acquired, my mother's was all natural ability. For years I based my perception of Lorraine's coolness on that left eyebrow. (My perception of just the opposite was based on my mother's left hook. Right-handed children are definitely at a disadvantage with a left-handed parent. Those left hooks catch you every time, because you forget! You're so busy looking across at the hand you *think* is going to do the smacking!)

"Yeah! Here, look in the hatch," Mom said excitedly, as she waved her hand at Luke to motion for the key. He reached in to turn off the ignition, got the keys out, and handed them to her.

"Your grandmother went and got all this stuff and insisted I drive it all the way up here. I told her, 'Mama, they have stores in DC. Why don't you just send money?' But you know Nettie. She does what she wants to do, and she wants to make sure 'her children' are eating. Look! There's canned foods and juice, cookies…"

My roomies were leaning into the hatchback with my mother, ooh-ing and aah-ing, and generally excited that we would be well fed for a little while. I stifled my territorial urges and just smiled wanly at them as they staked out which goodies they couldn't wait to devour. I was trying to get used to the idea that I had a CAR!

I had backed away from the vehicle a little to give them room, and so as not to be looking the gift horse in the mouth. Lorraine came over to me.

"How about that, huh?" she said, pretty proud of herself. "I'm going to be in all kinds of debt trying to pay two car notes, but I think every girl should have her own transportation. I just couldn't stand it when you had to go to that cabaret last year with that other boy just because he had a car." "*That other boy*" was anybody who wasn't A.J., in her book.

"Well, thanks, Ma."

Lorraine knit her brow (of course she could make *both* those suckers frown!). "That means all A's now, right?"

I could feel each pore under my arms under attack. This wasn't a *money, stuff, or territory* issue. What was going on?

"If *that's* what this means, then you can just take that car right on back to Indiana," I said in another uncharacteristically bold move.

"No, well, just do the best you can, then."

"I will."

"Okay. Well, come on, Luke!" she said to my brother, who was still in the car. "I'm staying at the Howard Inn, room 525. I'll be here until Sunday morning. All you have to do is get me to the airport then, okay?"

"Sure."

"All right then," she said, getting into the car. "I'll talk to you tomorrow."

Mom and Luke drove off, and the three of us resumed our walk home.

"How we gon' act now that we got a car?" Sheila speculated.

"Like you don't have one," I told them. They were pretty silent the rest of the walk home.

The next day, I went to the hotel to see my mother. I told her all about Nnarami, and wanted her to meet him, so I called. I asked him if he'd come by to meet my mom. He said he was busy. I told him we could come and get him or just stop by his place for a minute. He said he was busy. I insisted that it would be no trouble because we had a car. He was still busy, but told me to tell her hello.

"By the way, I had a talk with Derrick the other day," Rami said.

My heart started pounding, my armpits tingled. "Oh...really?"

"Don't ever do that again."

"No, Ma, he's pretty tied up. I told you what a good student he is. Very serious."

"Hrumph."

CHAPTER 21

All I can remember is a flurry of activity after I got the Dodge. We went to every club, every weekend, and took as many people with us as we could. Sigma Image: We're cute! We're cool! We can party!

We had been halfheartedly practicing for the Homecoming Step Show, but once I got the car, that just opened up a whole new world for us. We were able to drive to New Jersey to visit our competition-winning sorors, who taught us some really nice routines during our get-there-practice-all-night-and-roll-out sessions. Then we were running all over the DC Metropolitan area hunting for just the right costumes—ones that we could afford and that everyone could agree on. And in blue and gold, which are not very popular clothing colors.

We wanted to wear blue tank tops under the yellow jacket and pants sets we found, but some of us were big-chested and protested the lack of support since they couldn't wear bras underneath the tanks. So we settled on the only other thing we could find—lightweight blue mock turtleneck sweaters for some, and tanks, still, for others. Except the store didn't have enough of either style in the right sizes, so we just bought everything they had and ended up fighting over who would wear what when we got to the auditorium.

By the beginning of October I had pretty much given up. I hadn't even tried to complete an S cycle, and was constantly finding or feeding company. I was spending half of my time mooning over Nnarami and the other half cursing him for leaving me high and dry so suddenly and for so long, when I just *knew* he had to want me just as much as I wanted him. Sheila and Irene seemed to think so, too (*"Rami really does love Lynn,"* Sheila doodled while we talked), although one of his fraternity's little sweethearts seemed to be answering his phone more and more. On a whim, I decided to *just make some reservations.* I put an ad in the personals of the school paper using the special Greek nomenclature that said exactly who the parties to the message were.

5-A:
Either you're not playing fair, or I don't know the rules. Please, let's talk...
6-SGR

Rami was livid! I ran into him after his last morning class. He was on his way home, walking up Harvard Street rather briskly. I was right on his heels, pleading with him to talk to me. Finally, he did.

"I don't believe you would do something like that to me."

"What else could I do? You wouldn't talk to me."

"I cannot believe you did that. It's over."

Funny, but that didn't sound like news to me.

"What was so wrong with what I did?" I asked.

"I don't want to talk about it."

"Why?"

"I said it's over!"

"Please!"

"It's over."

"Okay, I know!" *Shit! I got his point. I wasn't that thick!*

"But can't we be friends?"

"You're no friend. People don't do things like that to friends."

"Things like what? Try to talk to them?"

"You are morally bankrupt!"

I stopped speed walking and just stared at him. *Morally bankrupt?!*

"Oh, now come *on*!" I ran to catch up with him, but I didn't know what else to say. My underarms were killing me.

"Nnarami!"

"Nnaramiiiii!" He acted like he didn't hear me.

"I love you," I said, not necessarily so that he would hear me. He started to turn his head, but changed his mind and kept walking. I turned and ran all the way back to campus.

The bro's threw a party that night. Irene, Sheila, Kern, Joy, Antoinette and I went wearing new matching T-shirts with our numbers on them. Bad idea. I saw Rami pointing me out to the sweetheart through the picture window of the frat house. We left the party early, and my sorors tried to console me.

Antoinette:	"I'm sorry, Joe."
Sheila:	"Don't worry about them."
Kern:	"But hey, you won't be needing that keychain anymore now, will you?"

That's right...Kern's *"Man Is An Alpha,"* too.

"Here, Kern."

"Thanks."

Sheila:	"Damn, bitch! Give her some time!"
Irene:	"He's an ass, Joe."
Joy:	"An *'astral?'* What did you say?"
Irene:	"To Joe: He's an *ass*. He's-an-*ass*,-Joe."
Joy:	"Oh! Yeah."
Sheila:	"And she's an ass, too."
Antoinette:	"No, it's not *her* fault, so she's not a *total* ass like he is."
Sheila:	"You're right. She's...uh...*half* an ass!"
Joy:	"A LITTLE ass."
Kern:	"Yeah, a little *ass*, all right!"
Antoinette:	"Kern!"
Kern:	"Sorry!"

"Ass-*ette*," Irene translated *into* French.

Sheila: "That's it! Ass and Assette."

But didn't that make it sound real cozy, like they belonged together?

CHAPTER 22

Homecoming arrived. We had a house full of people because some of the New Jersey sorors were there to step with us, and everybody had invited somebody up, down or over for the festivities. They were sleeping all over the floor in the living room, dining room, *our* rooms... We had to miss most of the Homecoming activities that day in order to practice. Our routine had nice steps, but sorry to say, DC Sigmas were not competition material. Most of us were just not cut out to perform.

For two days before the show, I was picking people up from the airport, running people around, going to stores, running, running, running... but finally the time was here.

After we finished fighting and determined who would wear the tank tops and who would wear the sweaters, there was about an hour left before the show with nothing to do.

"Should we practice?"

"Nope. Won't do much good now."

I looked around the dank little dressing area...and swooned.

My sorors screamed and caught me, easing me into a chair.

Antoinette:	"What's wrong? What's the matter?"
Kern:	"It's that hot-ass sweater y'all making her wear!"
Sheila:	"Her problem is she hasn't been eating."
Irene:	"I been telling her to slow down!"
Antoinette:	"Get her something to drink."
Sheila:	"Get her something to eat."
Kern:	"Get her out of that hot-ass sweater!"
Joy:	"Joe, you okay?"

Sheila: "Does she *look* okay?"
Joy: "Look, you don't have to get nasty!"
Irene: "Somebody go get her something!"

Joy stomped off.

Kern: "Let me go ask Rick."

Kern returned with a McDonald's bag with two cheeseburgers and fries in it. "I told the bro's what happened, and they sent this over."

I took a cheeseburger, unwrapped it and took a big bite.

"It's from Rami. He's concerned about you."

What's he doing eating McDonald's?

RAMI? I started rewrapping the burger to put it back in the bag.

"Stop being silly, Joe, and eat!" Sheila berated me. Then she leaned close and whispered, "He's *concerned.* Did you hear that?"

I'd heard, but I found it hard to believe, as much as I wanted to.

"I'm finished. I'm fine. I'll just have something to drink and everything will be okay." Joy had returned with a Coke.

"Sure?"

"Yeah! See?" I said, standing up. "Why don't we go ahead and practice a little?"

The six of us rounded up the additional seven sorors from New Jersey who were stepping with us, and went into a narrow back hallway to line up and quietly go through our routine.

I was on the end, so when a bunch of bro's came down the hallway and tried to squeeze past, I came face to face with Rami. That sweater sure was hot!

"How are you feeling?"

"Fine. Thanks for the food."

"No problem. Take care of yourself, okay?"

"I will."

Showtime!

Imitation being the sincerest form of flattery, sororities will often imitate fraternities during their step show performances. We did that, too, but in the interest of being novel, we poked a little fun at them by taking it a step further. We used canes in one step, as Kappa's do, but then dropped them all. Our Omega step was so wild and full of energy (like they are) that we ended up stomping all over each other. I can't remember what we did to imitate the Phi Beta's. The Bro's, though, because we had enjoyed such a closeness with them, were truly upset about our insinuation that they were "old and tired" when we fell out, exhausted, at the end of one of their popular steps.

We all dispersed after we performed, so we didn't hear any of the fallout that day. But we would!

We saw Derrick walking to campus that next Monday, and stopped to give him a ride.

"Sure, I'll take a ride, even though y'all wanna diss a brotha."

"What? Are you talking about the step show?" I asked.

"We weren't dissing anybody! It was all in fun!" Sheila protested. "But if it upset you, then we're *sorry*."

"Yeah? Well, I accept your apology, but you maybe need to tell the rest of the bro's."

"Are they really pissed?" Irene asked.

"Aw, man. 'Pissed' is not even the word."

We printed an apology in the school paper that week. Still, the advertisement for our next party was printed under the heading "For Sale." And nobody came.

I went to sit in the audience with Luke and my mother (who came to see me in my first step show). She met me

117

backstage after we finished stepping so that she could walk me back to her seat, and I could watch the rest of the show. I really wanted to see Nnarami. I couldn't imagine him stepping.

I spied him from a slight distance on our walk from backstage, where the Alpha's were still waiting to perform.

"Ma! There he is! That's Rami!"

"Where?"

"Over there! See? In the black and gold, *duh*."

"Him? Walking past that girl with the poster right now?"

"Yeah! That's him!"

"Oh, my God. He's ugly!"

?

"What?"

My mother chuckled. "Girl, you must be blind. He's hideous!"

"Uh-uhn!"

"Please! I don't know why you're wasting your time."

CHAPTER 23

A couple of days later, I came home and Sheila and Irene greeted me at the door. "Look what we *found* leftover from Homecoming, still wandering around campus!" An old flame, Dave, was sitting at the dining room table, so I just assumed he'd been *fed*, too. My girls were watching out for me…because A.J. was beginning to look a lot like Christmas!

We didn't say anything. Dave and I just grinned at each other, a testament to how much fun we'd had together. We used to categorize our kisses: cartoon, TV or movie, and then the movie kisses were further broken down by rating: G, PG, R, or XXX (and you have to *really* have good teeth for those!). I was so fond of him that I promised no matter who I married, I would always be willing to have an affair with him. Dave could be my "Mister" (masculine version of "mistress") any time, I told him.

So we went up to my room and *talked*, since Sheila and Irene and their other guests were still sitting in the dining room. Besides, *first* we had some unfinished business to discuss from the year before.

"What happened to you?" Dave questioned. "I woke up that last morning, and you were gone. No note, no call, no nothing!"

I woke up in his room that morning, sat on the edge of his bed and spied a photo album across the room. With nothing better to do until he got up, I looked through it. When I finished, I did something I hadn't done before in all my visits to Dave's room—I took the time to notice the hordes of photos all over his room that were just like the ones in the book. There were lovey-dovey, all-hugged-up, kissy-kissy photos…and posters, magnets, keychains, a mug, greeting cards, a couple of banners…Dave and his girlfriend and declarations of their deep and abiding love.

I had an epiphany.

At first I was sad. *Nobody is decorating their room with declarations of love and pictures of <u>me</u>.*
Then I was envious. *That's what I want, and I deserve it, too!*
Next I felt stupid. *Well, I'll never get it from a guy who already has his walls and his heart all filled up with another girl.*
Finally, I felt ashamed. This girl deserved *all* of his love, but Dave was spoiling it! and I was helping him by being available for him to cheat with.
I was wrong, dead wrong! Sadly, I knew that if not with me, then Dave would be cheating with somebody else. Well, it would have to be with somebody else! I figured I could do better than that! I didn't have to sneak a piece of somebody else's…somebody else's…well, a guy who cheats isn't worth anything…so, somebody else's *shit*.
I left that morning and didn't look back.
Dave said he guessed that's what had happened (I left the album open on his desk). He said he'd had an epiphany that day, too, and broke up with his girlfriend right after that! He told her honestly that he was at HU! where the ratio of women to men was a mind-boggling 7:1, and he didn't want to make promises to her—or anybody else—that he couldn't keep! Good for Dave!
So then we caught up on each other's summers and started reminiscing about our kisses...

The fire started right there on my bedroom floor and spread down the hall to the upstairs bathroom. From there it went back to the bedroom before snaking its way down the stairs. It was held up for a while on the landing and again at the bottom of the staircase. It blazed across the living room floor to make a little hot spot in the vestibule by the front door. Seeking uncharted territory, the fire rolled on through the dining room and kitchen to the sunroom at the back of the house. Then it retraced its path, stopping to burn up the downstairs powder room on its way back to the vestibule, before finally breaking down into its two separate and distinct elements—me and Dave.

I gave my Mister a cartoon kiss to see him off, closed the front door, and leaned against the short wall that separated the foyer from the living room. *<sigh>*

"Are you done yet? Can a Black man get some sleep ANYWHERE around here?"

"A.J.? That you?" I peeked around the corner. There *was* somebody sitting on the couch!

"Yes," he replied curtly.

"What are you doing down here?"

"Trying to get away from you."

"Sorry!" I laughed.

"No, you're not."

"You're right. I'm not! How long have you been there?"

"Long enough. Before that I was in my room trying to sleep. Couldn't do that, couldn't use the upstairs bathroom, so I came down here. Congratulations on breaking your little dry spell."

"Thanks! Six weeks—whew! Now it's your turn. It won't be right until everybody breaks the house in!"

"Yeah, well anyway, you need to get your naked ass on up to your room."

"*Riiiight,*" I responded, suddenly feeling very nude. "Close your eyes."

"Considering everything I've seen tonight, I don't see why I should have to!"

"A.J.!"

"All right. Go now. And *stay* there!"

CHAPTER 24

The design completed, materials purchased, and mattress borrowed (and sprayed, don't forget!), my brothers came over on each of three weekends to construct my loft.

In the basement, they laid out all the pieces of wood and marked where they would drill the holes for the screws.

"Screws? I want it nailed to the wall!"

"Stupid! What you gon' do when you move?" Luke argued.

"I told you, we're not going anywhere!"

"Hand me that drill, Luke." Bill was a no-nonsense kind of guy. It wasn't worth his time to get into a little tiff with me. He had gotten sensitive in his old age, especially since he got a wife who liked to pamper him. Bill swore the dust was killing him, so he worked with a mask on and the basement door open, complaining the whole time.

"When we get all these holes drilled, then we'll haul this stuff upstairs and put it together. Luke! Did that last hole go all the way through?" Bill was peering into the sawdust-filled hole he'd just made in a thick 4x4.

"I can't see…" Luke said from the other side of the post.

<WHOO!>

"Owww!"

"Oops! Sorry, man!"

"I'm dying here! Girl, you better appreciate this! Help me get these splinters out of my eye."

The engineers forgot to build a ladder, but we tried it out, and found that I could swing myself up onto the bed by way of a crossbeam and the closet door.

"This loft can support no more than—how much do you weigh?" Luke asked.

"One thirty."

"One hundred and forty pounds," Bill advised.

"Oh, I see what you're saying. But you know, with it not being *nailed to the wall*, I wouldn't dare have anybody up there, anyway!"

CHAPTER 25

Back in September, this security guard named Ray got my number when he stopped in at La Vie for lunch.

"Where you go to school?" he'd asked me.

"UDC." I didn't tell locals I went to Howard, just in case they had issues with "snooty" Howard people.

"Oh? What you takin' up?"

"Mortuary Science."

"Really? My cousin is a funeral director! His name is Tony Reed. How about I get your number so y'all can hook up or something?"

I gave Ray my number in September, and his "cousin" Tony only got around to calling in November. For some trash, too.

"Hello?"

"Hey...yeah, this Tony Reed. I got your number from Ray." He sounded distant, dry, and monotone.

"Oh, yeah! How are you?"

"Fine. Yeah, he said you were in Mortuary Science."

"Um hum. I started this past spring, and I'm taking one class this semester."

"Yeah, I know them people up there. You one of Mr. Crane's girls?"

Mr. Crane, the Chairman of the department, was rumored to have been some kind of womanizer in his day.

"No, but we're cool, though."

"Yeah, and Mr. Temple think he so fine. And Mrs. Truesdale. They call her 'Miss Cutie on Duty.' Yeah."

His point? I didn't say anything.

"Listen. Do me a favor. I'mmo put one of my buddies on the phone, and I want you to talk to him like you a white girl. Tell him you and your girlfriend are coming over."

"For what?" *Why was I even entertaining this?*

"We just playing a joke on him."

"I don't know..."

"Come on. You can do it. You sound just like a white girl."

"No, I do not!"

But I talked to his friend, who was under the impression that two white girls were going to come over and "play." I thought he was an ignorant fool, and this Tony person was really silly, too. He didn't even know me, asking me to do something silly like that. But what did I look like doing it?

Tony got back on the phone, laughing. "He bought it! Yeah, we gon' run out and leave him here waiting for some white girls." Tony thought this was very funny, indeed! Then he stopped laughing. "But I gotta get home early and get some sleep. I got a funeral in the morning."

I perked up at this. "Really?"

"Yeah. At 11:00. The wake was tonight."

"Oh. I was going to say, maybe I could come to it because I've got a paper to write. But I missed the wake. I guess I could make that part up, though, huh?"

"Yeah. You can come. Maybe I'll let you help me close the casket."

"Oh, cool! Yeah, I'll be there. Where is it?" I got all of the details and Tony's phone and pager numbers. I felt pretty good. This would be the last really good day to get the assignment done (Saturday) because it was due on Wednesday, and I would actually get to participate!

I had no sooner hung up when the phone rang again. It was Sheila, calling me from her room down the hall. We all had separate lines. Can you imagine if we didn't?

"Joe? Could you come to my room for a minute? I need to ask you something."

"Okay," I said, not thinking that she could have just asked me over the phone.

When I got to her room, Sheila said sweetly, "Could you turn off my light, please?"

She was so silly! I shook my head and went and sat on the edge of her bed. She was in it, but it was freshly made. Sheila couldn't go to bed on rumpled sheets. I told her about the conversation I'd just had with Tony.

"He seems weird, Joe. I don't know," Sheila said.

"Yeah, but I'm glad I'll get my paper done, and probably not too many people will be *in* their paper."

"You're right. And you know, he just may not have known how to approach you, so he did it all wrong. And stupid. But you never know. He might be cute. You might get to like him."

"Well, I'll say this. He's already in the profession I'm trying to get into, so he's going to be my friend whether I like him or not."

"That's cool. And you just never know," Sheila reminded me.

"Thanks. I'll let you know all about it." I turned off the Short Bitch's light, closed her door, then turned and walked down to the other end of the hall into the bathroom. Irene's rooms were right behind the bathroom, and I could tell she was home and had company. She was one of those loud women.

It was embarrassing sitting there listening to Irene screaming and carrying on, but when you gotta go, you gotta go. I started thinking about Nnarami, thinking about the last time we were together, two months before. Then I tried to imagine what kind of person Tony would turn out to be. Maybe Sheila was right; he probably just didn't know how to act. What if he wasn't trifling, but turned out to be nice—and cute, too? I was sitting on the stool so long that I did some business I hadn't gone in there to do.

"You never know," I said to myself, as I reached over and turned on the shower.

CHAPTER 26

I had no idea how I was going to find this boy. "I'll be wearing round, gold-rimmed glasses," he'd told me on the phone. That sounded like just about every other pseudo fly-guy in DC.

It was a beautiful Saturday morning for the middle of November. The sun was shining, there were puffy clouds in the sky, and it was pretty warm, even for 10:00 in the morning. The hair-frizzing humidity was gone with the summer, thank goodness, because even though most of my hair was safely in a bun, it was freshly shampooed. One thing I always liked about DC is the weather. The winters were usually pretty mild, and it was shaping up to be one of those mild winters.

I wandered in and out of New Southern Rock Baptist Church before the funeral began, trying to figure out which of these fly niggers was the fly nigger I was supposed to be meeting. I stopped a man who looked like a funeral director (what does a funeral director look like?).

"Are you the funeral director?"

"One of 'em." What did he mean, "one of them?" I thought there was only one, and then maybe some helpers.

"Is Tony Reed here?"

"I don't know who you talkin' 'bout."

"He's supposed to be directing the funeral, one of the funeral directors."

"Naw, I don't know who you mean. Go ask the fella over there," he said, pointing off in some vague direction.

"Thank you." *Ignorant ass.*

So I was looking for a *late*-ass, fly-ass nigger. I walked into the sanctuary and perched on the edge of a pew in the back row, trying to be unobtrusive, as if anybody could tell I didn't know this dead man they were about to eulogize. I pulled the folded assignment sheet out of the inside pocket of Luke's old suit jacket that I wore because I was trying to blend in and look like a funeral director myself. Instead, I looked like the tacky college girl that I was. I had on a black skirt, white shirt (Luke's again) with pearls, and that dark gray jacket. I felt tacky, too, especially with the big hole in my pantyhose right on my left thigh. I just prayed that it was a sturdy hole, one that wouldn't run.

"Attend a wake and funeral service and write a report detailing your experience. Pay attention to details..."

I thought about how I could fudge some information about the wake that took place the night before. Mrs. Truesdale, my Funeral Service Orientation teacher, wouldn't be at this gangster's wake or funeral. How would she know? (Because funeral service practices are regional, and I would say some things that don't happen in Washington, DC!)

I looked at my watch. It was 10 minutes to 11:00. Everybody knows that funerals start precisely on time. They are the one thing that generally aren't affected by "C.P. time." Right then, two men came backing down the center aisle, pulling the casket. On the other end were two men pushing. One had on a three-quarter-length overcoat and round, gold-rimmed glasses. When they got the casket to the front of the church, he darted back up the aisle to the dry-ass funeral director I had talked to. The one who didn't know him.

I stood and walked over to where they were standing. I smiled.

"Tony Reed?'

"Yeah, hi. Nice to meet you. Sorry I'm late. The body was leaking." He said all of this while giving me a limp handshake.

"Leaking? Where?" This would be great for my paper.

"Here," Tony said, pointing all over his skinny chest. He was shot up."

Tony was thin, and only about an inch or so taller than my own 5'6". He was light skinned with a big, square head. And he had some huge teeth (two of them on the side overlapped—ugh) that I saw when he smiled, or leered, or whatever it was he did. It was like the puppet in that old, old horror movie "Magic." You know, his lips kind of curled back and changed shape or something. It was ugly, but he looked shiny and clean, so I could see how someone might find him attractive, just not me. *Oh well.* I remembered my promise to befriend him, and tried not to show my disappointment. Who was I kidding? I was hoping I'd find somebody to replace Nnarami.

I scribbled the leakage information on the assignment sheet. (Later I would learn that there was no reason for a body to leak from the chest.)

"Can you show it to me? I need to get a look at the body anyway."

"Sure, come on."

I checked out the floral displays and took notes as we walked down the center aisle. I was really giving myself away now. There were lots of pretty sprays, and what I know now is the standard "bleeding heart." That's a heart-shaped arrangement of white carnations with a few red ones dripping down the middle like blood. It usually comes from someone like the mother or the girlfriend. Then there was this clever guitar-shaped arrangement. I guessed that our man, Leon (I was up close and reading some of the cards by now) was a musician as well as a drug-dealing gangster.

I completely forgot to take note of what kind of casket Leon reposed in, probably because I wouldn't have known what to say about it, anyway, besides what color it was. But I guess the color was a complement of brown, because that's what color suit dude had on. And an animal print tie. Ugh.

Leon was the same color as his suit, and he looked just like any other brother walking the streets of DC. I couldn't tell by looking at his shirt that he had been leaking Lord-knows-what just a few minutes earlier.

"Maybe I'll let you hold the flowers while I close the casket."

"Oh, okay." *Cool!*

We walked back up the aisle and I, not knowing what else to do right then, sat back down on my pew when Tony said, "I'll be right back." The next time I saw him, ten minutes later, he was walking in behind the minister and three other funeral directors who were escorting Leon's closest relatives.

"I am the resurrection and the life: he that believeth in me, though he were dead, yet shall he live: And whoever liveth and believeth in me shall never die," the minister preached as he lead the troupe towards brother Leon. I sat there feeling stupid because I thought I was going to be walking up front to hold the flowers. I watched Tony. When the family started seating themselves in the first few pews (wrong!), he walked back up the left aisle of the church. He looked as if he was going to keep walking out the door, but I stopped him.

"Tony!" I half-whispered.

He rolled over to my pew and sat next to me.

"I got bumped out," he said. "Everybody wants to showboat today." He had apparently forgotten his promise of 15 minutes earlier, to let me hold the flowers.

"What's that?" I asked.

"Did you see that guy bump me out of the procession? They up there fighting over who's gon' close the casket."

Nobody looked like they were fighting to me. One man stood at the head, another at the foot, and a third man was right in the middle, ushering the family members by. Then, when the last person had viewed the body, the middle man turned and lifted the casket spray high in the air and held it there. The old man at the foot came around to the front and took the overlay off the foot panel of the casket, folded it, and placed it on Leon's chest, careful not to cover his face. The family members, who were already crying, started to get agitated. Then the old guy at the head of the casket came around to the front and folded the skirt over into the casket. This covered Leon's face a little, and the top of his head.

"No, Lord, you can't take my baby!" cried Leon's mother. I tapped an old woman who looked like a church missionary.

"Can I look at your program for a minute? I asked?

"I need it back, honey."

"Oh, yes. I just want to look for a minute," I told the program monger.

Leon's mother's name was Abigail. Abigail? How do you get a name like that?

So Abigail was all distressed, and she started distressing everybody else. The man who was at the head released the joint holding the lid of the casket up with his left hand, and slowly began to lower the lid with his right hand. The Johnston clan went wild!

"Don't close the casket! No! Take me!" All the young woman had to do was pitch forward from her seat in the first pew in order to snatch the old man and try to stop him from closing the lid. Two family men from the front pew grabbed her arms and dragged her back the two feet to the bench and sat her down. No sooner than her butt hit the seat, another woman was up and running, rushing the poor old man who had just gotten his balance back from the first attack.

"Let me see him! I want to see him! He ain't dead! Don't close it, he can't breathe! Leon! Leon!" Abigail looked like she was about ready to faint. She swooned in her seat. Women gathered around and fanned her while the rest of the first pew crew grabbed the second attacker and dragged her back.

The old guy made quick work of closing that casket then. The flower guy put the casket spray back down and turned around. One director walked up the left aisle, one up the center, and the third, up the right aisle. They met at the back of the church and went out into the vestibule.

"I'll be right back, " Tony said, and slid out of the pew and through the doors to join his colleagues.

Maybe because Leon was a musician, he had lots of artistic friends. Maybe that's why all the theatrics at his funeral that day.

After the Scripture and Prayer, Alice Hines sang *"His Eye Is On The Sparrow."* Luckily she had a strong voice and a mike because the crying was so loud.

> *Why should I feel discouraged?*
> *And why should the shadows come?...*
> *When Jesus is my portion,*
> *My constant friend is he,*
> *His eye is on the sparrow*
> *And I know he watches me.*

About three people left the sanctuary before Sister Alice even got really cranked up.

> *I sing because I'm happy,*
> *I sing because I'm free.*
> *His eye is on the sparrow,*
> *And I know he watches me.*

By the time she finished, Alice had about 15 people in the back of the church acting a fool!

Things did not get any better. The minister preached about senseless tragedies and told the people they needed to get saved right now! It was the organist who reeled everybody in, though. He must have been a direct descendant of The Pied Piper. He was working the volume pedal, up and down, up and down. Up (Daaaa)—down!(da!)

Minister: "Because I know—"
　　　　　　Organist: Daaaa da!

Minister: "That the Lord—"
　　　　　　Organist: Daaaa da!

Minister: "Is my Shepherd—"
　　　　　　Organist: Daaaa da!

Minister: "I believe—"
　　　　　　Organist: Daaaa da!

Minister: "That He will—"
　　　　　　Organist: Daaaa da!

Minister: "Lead me home—"

　　　　　　(upbeat organ intro)
　　　　Da da dum da da da da da da!

Precious Lord, take my hand,
Lead me on, let me stand.
I am tired, I am weak, I am worn!

A guy on the left side of the church jumped straight up out of his seat, about three feet in the air, stiff and straight like this exclamation point: ! He did that four times in a row and then calmly sat back down. They carried a little girl who looked like she might be Leon's six-year-old niece, Crystal, out of the church. Women were dancing in the aisles. One of them stopped dancing and fell over sideways, stiff like the jumping man. They carried her out of there, too, laid out like Leon.

I was trying not to laugh. When was this circus going to be over? Mrs. Truesdale was going to love this paper! Where the heck was Tony? I got up and went out into the vestibule with the crazies, who were calmer out here without so much of an audience. About ten minutes later, Tony came smiling and strolling up to me with yet another one of the directors.

"Where have you been?"

"We went for some breakfast." The nerve! I was starving. And they could have been late getting back or anything. What was wrong with this guy?

"Oh." Then we just stood in the vestibule for a while. It emptied out after the singing. Then people started passing through the vestibule, going downstairs, when all the deacons in Leon's mama's church got up to speak (two minutes each). For a while, at least, everything was calm.

But not outside. Something was brewing. About five police cars pulled up on the street. "What's that all about?" I asked Tony.

"They expecting some trouble. Maybe even a shoot-out!"

"A shoot-out! What should we do?"

"Nothing. Just stay here and wait. Right by the door."

The police kind of milled around outside, not looking particularly concerned about anything. Then, suddenly, a man pulled open the outside doors and strode inside. He was a little grungy looking and wore a long, dirty trench coat, which he closed in front of him by putting his hands in the pockets, which were bulging considerably.

My heart started pumping fast, and I could feel the sting in my armpits as the sweat broke through when he flung open the doors of the church, hands still in his pockets, and walked purposefully down the center aisle. A plainclothes policeman ran into the vestibule just as the dirty man unhooked the barrier that prevented anyone from going near the casket or the family in the first few pews. The man didn't bother to hook it back behind him. He seemed to be in a hurry.

The cop had stopped right at the door where I was standing, and we all just watched as the man reached the first pew. The family looked up, alarmed, but then Abigail scooted over and let him sit next to her. Whew! He was okay!

Everyone in the vestibule breathed a sigh of relief. I told Tony that I was going to sit down, and eased into the sanctuary and reclaimed my back pew seat. Shortly, though, the service was over. The minister was calling for the morticians. Tony came in and asked if I wanted to ride in the flower car with him. Of course I did! Maybe this is what he'd meant by me helping with the flowers, not up at the casket.

As several young ladies carried flowers out of the church, we took them and put them into a hearse. We got them all loaded and left for the cemetery before they even brought Leon out of the church.

"We'll take these flowers to the cemetery, then I gotta go get my car, and I'll take you back to the church so you can get your car, okay?

"That's fine," I told Tony. We started to chit-chat a little then.

"Do you go to church?" he asked.

"Well, not really. I mostly go to bible study, where you can learn things."

"Yeah, I just started getting into the Word myself."

"Really?" Maybe he would turn out to be a good guy after all!

"Yeah. I lost a few people I was really close to, and then I just went through some bad times. It makes me feel better when I read about the love of God, you know, and see how other people suffered, but trusted in Him to make things all right."

"Umm..." I didn't want to get into a discussion about religion right then.

We got to the cemetery, found the plot that went with our service, and unloaded the flowers. We ran back and forth from the driveway up a hill to the grave, arranging the sprays around the bier and the tent. Pumps are not the shoes to wear in a cemetery. My heels kept sinking into the ground. I imagined people getting poked in the eye beneath me. *Oops! Sorry, Mr. Montrell. Pardon me, Mrs. Rollins. Hee, hee.*

"Just in time. Here they come!"

I looked in the direction Tony was looking in and could see a long line of cars making its way toward us. "Let's get out of here," Tony said.

"Aren't we staying for the INTER-ment?" I asked, pronouncing the word wrong. It came out sounding like "enter" plus "mint." Tony laughed. I thought that was rude.

"What did you say?"

"You know, the burial."

"In-TER-ment," he enunciated, still laughing. "Nah, I need to get back."

"All right." I was a little disappointed (yet again), but figured I would just make up this part of my paper, too. I figured I had been to enough funerals at home in Indiana (except I didn't know that in the DC area, wakes don't go on all day, and caskets aren't normally lowered at the cemetery). So we ran down the hill (me on my toes), jumped into the hearse, and sped away out of Franklin National Cemetery.

CHAPTER 27

Tony's car was some little red, sporty-looking thing, but it was old, banged-up, and dirty. It wasn't even his. "I'm just borrowing Ray's car for a while," he explained as he fumbled around the ignition with a screwdriver. The car started.

"Do you want something to eat?" he asked. I didn't have any money on me, so I hoped he was treating.

"Sure. Ah, *your* treat, *my* treat, or *dutch* treat?" It was only polite to ask.

"I got you. How about that Wendy's up there?"

We went through the drive-through, and then Tony suggested that perhaps I would like to go back to his place and eat, since it wasn't far. I agreed to this.

Tony lived on the third floor in a complex of garden-style apartments on Iverson Street in Prince George's (PG) County, Maryland. There was little in the way of furniture in the place. Upon entering the apartment, there was a weight bench and a set of weights on the left, a small stereo rack system, and a big, empty ceramic elephant planter. On the right was a glass and brass dining table with four black velvety upholstered chairs. There was one of those three-part pictures on the wall with a contrived scene of a bunch of pink flowers wrapped in tissue paper and ribbon, and scissors and clippings laying all around. Behind the dining room was the kitchen, with a huge microwave sitting on the counter.

Straight ahead through a doorway was the bathroom, decorated with a burgundy shower curtain and three-piece carpet ensemble for the toilet and floor. Ray's room was to the right of this, and Tony's room was to the left, facing the parking lot.

We made quick work of the fast-food supper, but Tony didn't look like he was ready to take me back to DC to my car just yet. In fact, he was getting quite comfortable, having taken off his suit and put on some pajama bottoms, a T-shirt, and some fuzzy red footies. I hadn't seen a pair of footies in ages, and I had never seen a man wear any. He invited me into his bedroom, which is where I guessed he entertained his company, not having any furniture besides the dining table.

I sat at the foot of the bed, my face just a few feet from a large, wooden entertainment center with a 19-inch color TV, a VCR, and an ugly Siamese cat statue. The other half of the entertainment unit held a stuffed rabbit and two framed photographs of women who did not look like Tony, but whom he claimed were cousins.

There was a nightstand on the far side of the bed, near the wall with the window looking out at the parking lot. A lamp with three round globes at different heights sat on the table. On the near side of the bed was a box wrapped in Christmas paper with a stack of old-looking books sitting on top of it. The closet was on the wall next to this.

In an arch above the headboard were about ten more framed pictures of women, and at least one of them was photographed in her underwear in what she must have thought was a seductive, yet tasteful pose. She was cute, but she had a mustache.

Tony went into Ray's room for a few minutes and then returned. I thought maybe I should have said hello or something to Ray since I knew him first, after all, but I didn't feel like it.

"You can get comfortable if you want," Tony said.

"Thanks," I said, taking my jacket off. Tony hung it up in his closet, then pulled out a stiff, red, white, and blue satin robe. "Kick your shoes off. Here, you can put this on."

My brain hadn't kicked into action yet as I took the robe from him and put it on over my skirt and shirt. I tied it, then guessing that I was still not comfortable enough, slipped out of my skirt and pantyhose. That run was bothering me.

Meanwhile, Tony was fooling around with the TV and VCR. "Do you want to watch a movie?" he asked.

Cinema. "Sure. What movie?"

But he didn't have to answer because the movie was on. Some white woman dressed in a fake-me-out tuxedo outfit was poking around in an empty nightclub. She settled down on a high stool in front of the bar, and a big, dirty-looking man approached her and promptly tore off the skimpy little shorts she had on. He started ramming his whole fist into her.

I was fascinated. I had only seen one other blue movie before, and I started running my mouth.

"He's got his whole hand inside her! She looks pretty silly with her shoes still on. Ooh, look! How did the camera get in there? Oh, that looks painful! Oh, that's interesting. What do you call that?"

Tony climbed onto the bed, right where I was sitting, which means he climbed right on top of me. I slid back towards the headboard. "Hey! I'm trying to see this." Admittedly, watching that movie was pretty exciting, what with my dry spell just recently over and all. But Tony was far from exciting. He kept coming at me, though, kissing my neck, my cheeks, my lips. Finally, I gave in and parted my lips for one deep, sensuous kiss, thinking that would satisfy him. It didn't.

By now I couldn't see the movie at all. Tony was on his knees over me, untying the robe and stroking my breastlets through my bra. Then his hands were under my bra and he was still kissing me. Well, after I let him kiss me once, how could I say no to another...and another...and...

Then he lowered his body on top of mine. I had been propped up on my elbows, but they slid out from under me. I had nowhere else to put my hands except on or around his back, which I did, and closed my eyes and just enjoyed the kisses. Then Tony shifted and his thigh rubbed against my pelvis. An electric current raced around that area and I caught myself pressing back against him.

"No, Tony. Stop it!"

"Stop what?" he asked quietly, moving his mouth from my exposed left nipple just long enough. His hand quickly slid down the left side of my body and into my panties, finding it quite wet down there. How embarrassing!

"Stop. I don't know you!" I slid back a little farther on the bed. He slid up, too, removing his hand but grinding his hips into mine. He was hard. He kissed me again, stopping my protesting.

"It's okay. I know what I'm doing."

"Well, I don't, and I said stop."

"All right," he said, and then he started moving his hardness against my wetness. My panties were soaked, and my body was feeling, well, very good.

"'All right?'" I repeated, then I couldn't help laughing because he had said 'all right' and then flat-out ignored me. Then he was taking off his pajama bottoms. "You're a baaad boy." That came from the movie. I thought about Nnarami, damn him.

"You like it," he said.

I didn't answer that. "Do you have anything?" I asked, trying to relax a little bit as he removed my panties and started pushing against my bare skin.

"No."

"No? Stop it! We can't!"

"It's okay. Nothing's going to happen." He was inside me now.

"Stop it, Tony! Stop!"

It was too little too late. He had already taken about five strokes by the time I finished saying that.

And it was feeling so good. I tried not to think about Nnarami or anybody as I pressed my heels into Tony's butt with all the urgency born from the need to forget and move on. We went on like that until I was tired, which was right around the time he pulled out and ejaculated all over my stomach.

Tony turned his back to reach for a small hand towel that had been on the nightstand the whole time. He deftly cleaned himself, then offered the towel to me to wipe up the spill. Then he got up, put on his robe, and left the room.

I just sat there and cried quietly on the inside, I'm sure.

CHAPTER 28

The next day, Sunday, my sorors and I decided to go out for breakfast, and that found us in Tony's neighborhood. Suddenly PG County was a huge factor in my life! Several times I left the table to call or page Tony to see if he'd like to join us, but he was unavailable. I say "unavailable" because we didn't know if he was screening his calls or what. He was just unavailable.

"I went horseback riding," he told me when I finally talked with him later that evening. (Mind you, in all the years I knew him after that, he never went horseback riding again.)

"Oh, really?"

"Yeah."

"Well, I wanted you to meet my friends," I pouted.

"Some other time, maybe."

"Can I come over?"

"Ahh, well...sure."

"Good. I'll just pack a couple of things…"

"You're staying?"

"That's okay, isn't it?"

"I guess."

"I don't quite remember how to get over there. Why don't you meet me halfway?"

So we agreed to meet at a gas station halfway, and I would follow Tony home from there. I was at the gas station for about two hours before he showed up with some lame excuse. Not surprisingly, this happened often. I'd call and say I was coming over, but when I arrived, no one would answer the door. I'd drive to a pay phone, and if he answered, he'd swear he didn't hear me, or if he didn't answer at all, I'd have to drive back home.

The next morning after sex and while we were making up the bed together, Tony asked why I'd wanted to see him again. And do you know what I said?

"I'm looking for a husband." *I sure had a funny way of showing it, giving tail away!*

"Well, I'm looking for a wife." *So did he, conducting horizontal interviews.*

We both were quiet for a minute.

"You'd marry somebody like me?" I asked him. *Somebody like what? Somebody who gives tail away!*

"I guess so. Would you marry somebody like me?" *Somebody like what? Somebody who conducts horizontal interviews!*

"I suppose. It depends—would you go back to Indiana with me?"

"Maybe."

"Cool."

A week after that, we had our second party at the house. It was a bust. Again, nobody but the DJ showed up. Tony came, and stayed over. I could tell my sorors and A.J. didn't think much of him. A.J. simply ignored him. Sheila and Irene passive-aggressively showed me how they felt about my guest. They played the gracious hostess roles, while seating Tony in the odd chair at the dining table, giving him the odd plate with the odd silverware, and the odd, chipped teacup. I figured they were all just being loyal to Nnarami, so I couldn't fault them for that.

The day after that was my half-birthday (so it was six months after I'd run away from home). I love my birthday, did I tell you? So much that I found a way to celebrate it twice every year—by celebrating on the half. So I had a half-birthday party. I bought invitations and cut them in half. Ordered half a sheet cake. Decorated half of the living room. Nnarami was invited, and I waited breathlessly, but he didn't come.

The party was nice, anyway. I invited CoCo, a neighbor's cocker spaniel, and she came with her owner. Luke came, and cozied up with Carla, as they had been spending a loooot of time together. The highlight of the party was when CoCo decided she loved Luke. She ran circles around Carla and then back and forth to the front door in some sort of doggie hex.

After the party, we all went out to a club where the Alpha's were hosting a party. Nnarami was there. He told me I looked nice! He told my sorors he wanted to dance with me, but he never asked. We stared at each other from across the room most of the night. And then we all went home.

Later that week, Frank called me and A.J. into his office at La Vie.

"First of all, I want you guys to know you're doing a great job."

A.J., who was already standing almost on top of me, pressed even closer to my side in a subtle nudge.

"It's odd, though. It seems like we're as busy as we've ever been, but lately the place is just not showing the same profits it used to. Catering has been fine, but the owners have decided that since the store isn't pulling its weight, they're closing up shop."

"Wow..."

"So we're out of a job," A.J. clarified.

"'Fraid so, kiddo," Frank said, chucking me on the chin and then reaching out to pull me into a hug, which meant I practically had to sit on his lap. So I just sat there.

"Well, how long do we have?"

"End of the year."

"Gee, that's just about six weeks."

"You guys'll be okay, though. You're smart, you're great workers, you're good looking," Frank said, giving me a little squeeze for emphasis.

"Yeah, we're cool," A.J. said, pursing his lips in that annoyed look of his. "Come on, Joe. We need to get ready for the after-work rush."

"That's my girl," Frank said, giving me another squeeze for the road.

That evening, A.J. and I couldn't wait to close up our registers and get out of La Vie so that we could discuss this turn of events.

"Man, A.J., you've really done it this time!"

"What do you mean?"

"You put La Vie out of business!"

"I didn't do it by myself!"

"Oh, yes you did!"

"Come on, now, Joe. You helped. Hell—in fact, you started it!"

"I might have started it, but you perfected it!"

"Yeah, I did, didn't I?" A.J. succumbed to his smugness. "You were just nickel and diming, a penny-ante thief."

"Riiiiiight...I was happy skimming $10 a day."

"Man, they messed up when they put ME on the cash register!"

"I know!"

"That's why they shoulda paid me more than minimum wage. Then I wouldn't have to supplement my income."

"You call $300 a day a *supplement?*"

"Yeah, because it could have been more than that."

"But you had to leave *something* in the register."

"You know where you messed up? Not doing it during the lunch rush and actually trying to ring people out."

"I'm usually next door at the bar with Frank after lunch. And in his office hung over after that."

"Yeah, well, coffee and doughnuts in the morning don't add up as fast as lasagna priced by the pound. And while I've got the register open, ma'am, that cake is $30 with tax!"

"Hey! How did you get the price for the meals without putting them on the register scale?"

"I didn't. I just eyeballed it and gave people a deal. 'That will be $5.00.' They knew it cost more than $5.00, but of course they're happy to pay the bargain price."

"You know, though, it was hard keeping up with the money I was keeping in the drawer. I'm sure a lot of times I left some of it in the register, but the owners never said anything."

"They wouldn't. Would you? Just be glad you were never even a nickel short."

CHAPTER 29

I had been sleeping with Tony for about a month when I noticed something pretty special. I was having orgasms!

I once went on a date where afterwards, the guy wanted to make out. He was rubbing my stuff through my panties—about all I was letting him do, because I really wasn't digging on him too much—when I felt this build-up of heat down there (it definitely did not tickle!). Then it was like these "waves of liquid fire" spilled out all over my lap!

But I didn't believe I'd had an orgasm because I didn't know what they were and I didn't think I could have one that easily. And I didn't want to acknowledge that my first one was with that creep. The first couple of times I had them with Tony, I couldn't bring myself to believe it was really happening. Plus, the waves seemed to *splash* out, unlike that first slow, controlled spill.

"You know what?" I asked him one morning. "I think I had an orgasm last night. I...came!" I said, trying out the lingo.

"I know. I made you do it," he stated matter-of-factly.

"When you... touched my stuff while we were doing it?"

"Yep. I felt you come."

"You could feel it?"

"I mean, not with my hand. I felt it inside you."

"How'd you know how to do that?"

"I don't know...I guess...maybe my father told me or something."

"Oh, well, whatever. Just—thanks!"

"You're welcome," Tony chuckled.

Tony always made sure I had an orgasm, and more than that, his goal was to have one *with* me, at the same time. Soon (okay—immediately), I couldn't imagine sex without an orgasm. What would be the point? When I thought about all the guys who'd had sex with me and hadn't cared enough to make me come, or even inquire if I had or not, I felt...*pissed*. Pissed *off*, pissed *in*, pissed *on*... Clearly, I'd been used! Obviously, none of them really loved or cared about me like they said they did. Or they just didn't know what the hell they were doing! But what about a guy whose goal is to make sure *you* feel good? You gotta love a guy like that!

Right?

CHAPTER 30

I dropped out of school. I was hardly going to classes at Howard, and I certainly was not enjoying them, so I decided to just concentrate on the one course I was taking at UDC. I was miserable every time I passed by Howard's campus, and because I drive by habit, I passed HU on my way to everywhere. I still felt a sense of attachment and belonging, but I felt like a failure. I felt like I was missing out on something. I would cry if I passed by and heard the bell in the clock tower above Founder's Library tolling noon or 6 pm. That's when it would also play the school hymn, at the end of which we'd always wave, like good-bye.

> *When from thee we've gone away*
> *May we strive for thee each day*
> *As we sail life's rugged sea*
> *Oh, Howard, we sing of thee!*

Luke took some vacation time and we drove home for Christmas. Carla went with us so that she could meet our family and see Gary, Indiana. Not that there was much to see in a city that is on the verge of dying out, but that was exactly the reason to be excited—Gary had nowhere to go but up!

Going home was always a treat! I'd walk in the house, drop my stuff at the door, and begin prowling. Mom usually had something new for us to discover: new paint, rearranged furniture, new carpet, new dishes, food in the refrigerator...

The entire house had been remodeled! It looked like a charming country inn, which was nice... but we wanted to show Carla where we grew up, and this place wasn't it! Where was Luke and Bill's old trundle bed? Indeed, where was their bed*room*? It had been turned into a den. My room had turned into a fancy, chiffon-covered boudoir with framed Picasso prints instead of Wham! and Michael Jackson posters hanging on the walls (upside down so that I could look at them lying in bed). Where were our knick-knacks, our books, our old toys…? Luke was a Taurus, too, so he was having the same deep-seated problems I was having. He didn't even have a *room* anymore, and neither of us could find our stuff!

"It looks great, ma!"

"Yeah, real cool!"

But Carla was taken with all the pink, the lace, and the flowers, and especially the eclectically decorated room with two different paints and two differently wallpapered walls. Mom was flattered.

We went next door to greet grandma, who had dinner waiting for us. Carla stuffed herself and had to "rest for a spell" on the couch with one hand on her forehead and one on her stomach. Grandma was flattered.

The next day, we visited our father. Dad realized he and Carla had the same birthday. She called him "dad." He grinned.

Everywhere else we went, Carla was happy to greet the people, who she said were much friendlier than people on the East Coast. I started taking notice, and decided that she was right. People would smile and greet you, and even joke around with you in a carryout in a bad neighborhood at 2:00 am! So, Carla loved our hometown, and it loved her back. She sang "Gary, Indiana" from "*The Music Man*" to everyone, and sad to say, most of them hadn't even heard of the song, let alone the musical that put us on the map. They thought she made it up!

How cute!
That's so sweet!
That would make a good rap!

Making introductions was a little awkward. We couldn't figure out if Carla should be billed as *my* friend or Luke's *girlfriend*.

The only misstep Carla made, she made because she thought *we* were making things up. One of my girls stopped by, and Carla insulted her by refusing to believe me when I introduced my friend as Billie Jean—looking just like Janet, and last name Jackson to top it all off.

"That's not really your name, is it?"

"And my father's name is Jesse, too, so what? Man, if I'da known I had to *copyright* my shit…"

Carla blinked. "Well, *pardon me*…but you tart den a mongfecky!"

They got along famously.

While I was away, Sheila and Irene somehow talked A.J. into the basement. *("You can paint and fix it up really nice down there. Have your own entrance and everything!")* A girl from Sheila's job, Natalie, moved in.

I didn't think it would work, having a local-yokel living with us, but Natalie seemed cool. True to urban style, she wore lots of leather, jewelry and hair pieces, and she did her own nails (and ours!) as well as the experts. Plus, she was quiet and didn't mind all the antics in our house.

When I got back to DC, Tony gave me a sweater identical to one he'd gotten for himself. It was just sitting in a plain brown shirt box, not wrapped, not even under any tissue paper. I suspected a 2-for-1 after-Christmas sale, but it was the thought that counted, I suppose.

CHAPTER 31

It was time to revamp our house rules, or rather, invent some more fun!

Irene decided we needed quotas.

"Sheila's got this thing for Kappa's, Joe has got it bad for Alpha's, and I love Que's. But look, we can't have it looking like they're just passing us around. We gotta have limits. We need quotas."

"What are you saying? We can't date any more Kappa's, Alpha's, and Que's? I'm not dating any Phi Beta's!"

"No, I'm not saying that. I'm saying we should maybe only date two guys from each frat."

"Ever?"

"Ever."

"Two?"

"Only two."

"Well, I've reached my quota already."

"Me, too."

"Okay, then, *from here on out*, it's two."

"What's the penalty if we go over?"

"Basically, your *reputation*, Sigma *Image…*"

"Shit! Why somebody always gotta go dragging Sigma into this?"

There were two variations of the Sigma Gamma *Roll.* One was an entrance and exit policy for the shower. Once the shower was on, it just made sense that everybody take a turn…just keep it going until we were all finished. When one person rolled out, another was ready to roll in without turning the water off.

The other Sigma Gamma *Roll* was an entrance and exit policy for the car.

The Sigmobile stopped for no one! I'd slow waaay down, and the passenger had to jump, or *roll,* out. If someone in the back wanted to take the place of the person who had just rolled out of the passenger seat, they had to roll out and then back in, too.

My housemates had the technique down (because I taught them the *physics* of it—ha haaaa!), but one day Dave had a little trouble. He was in town and we were dropping him off at a friend's dorm. He rolled out of the Sigmobile, and Sheila rolled into his vacant seat in the front—but not before we rolled over his foot because he didn't get out of the way in time!

Then there was the Sigma Gamma *Stroll,* a special line dance we'd do at parties when just the right music was playing.

Sigma *Name-a* Rho was the phenomenon by which everyone obtained a new moniker. The nicknames just kind of happened to anyone who spent time at the house:

1. Sheila was "E" (from "Sheila E-la"); her guy was "Dog."

2. Irene was "Bean" (short for "Reney Beany"); her guy was "B-head."

3. Carla was "Shaka Zulu," and I was her "Squaw."

4. New housemate Natalie was "Betty" (short for "Fly Betty")

5. My Gary military college friend Robert was "Plebe," formerly known as "Frick."

6. Robert's friend Jamie was "Frick," formerly known as "Frack."

7. "Kool-Aid" was a chick who got her name from the stupid grin on her face when I walked in on her and A.J. (*Touché!*)

8. "Paul" just *looked* like a Paul, so we all fooled around and forgot his *real* name!

9. We figured we'd try out *A.J.'s* real name, but A.J. was not playing. "Wisely, not one of you has ever even *asked* what 'A.J.' stands for," he said, and he left it at that. Surprisingly, so did we.

10. We even tried to rename Tony.

"Magic," I suggested, thinking of the movie and that frightful, lecherous, puppet's smile.
"Shorty."
"Ummmm…ha! Never mind."
"Y'all can just call me by my first name," Tony offered.
"What—Anthony?"
"Nah. It's *Kevin.* Kevin Anthony Reed."

Carla packed her stuff and moved to Luke's the very next day.

CHAPTER 32

The grocery store did close at the end of December, so I was in need of work. I answered an ad that said I could make $1600 a month, no experience needed. It turned out to be selling encyclopedias. We had to go every day and learn a script. Then we went out into "the field," knocking on doors. They took us way out into the *sub*-uburbs, left us for about 6 hours, and then picked us back up. If we wanted to use the bathroom, we had to get into a person's good graces and into their apartment.

I went out with the crew one day, my first day out on my own, the day I was supposed to finally be added to payroll after two weeks of training, and I was really tired. It was frigid out—bone-chilling cold. I had on torn jeans, tennis shoes with no socks, a T-shirt, and a light jacket (all Luke's except for the shoes). I was hungry. I had no money. I felt ill. So when they dropped me off at an apartment complex in near-rural Virginia, I walked down some stairs where there were a bunch of cats hanging out and debris blowing around. Huddled in a corner away from the wind, I slept until they came to pick me up again.

I did not return the next day. Instead, I opened up the Yellow Pages and called every funeral home in town, asking to meet the person the funeral home was named for. In most cases, he was deceased himself. That's one of life's ironies—dead funeral directors. And dead ministers.

"Benjamin Hastings Funeral Home. May I help you?"

"May I speak to Mr. Hastings, please?"

"Ah...Mr. Hastings is deceased. May I help you?"

"Well, can I speak with the funeral director?"

Exasperated with me now. "The funeral director? Hold on." I supposed that was like calling a hospital and asking for the doctor.

"Bishop," said a bothered-sounding, rather gruff voice

"Hello, Mr. Bishop. My name is Lynn Joseph, and I'm a Mortuary student at UDC. I'd like to come by and meet you just to talk and get a feel for funeral service in this area since I'm not from here. I'm from Indiana."

"We don't have any openings at this time."

"That's fine. I'd just like to talk."

"Could you call back next week?"

After three similar phone calls, I caught on and one time I got lucky. A director's name was listed in the ad. "Hi. Is Jackie Anderson available?"

"Oh," the secretary said sweetly, and then called my bluff because I had used the woman's last name as if I didn't know her, "are you calling about the typing position?"

"Ah, yes. Yes, I am."

"Well, when can you come in for an interview?"

"I can come any time."

"How about tomorrow at 1:00?"

"That will be fine."

"Great! Your name again?"

"Lynn Joseph."

"All right, Lynn. You'll be meeting with Miss Warner tomorrow at 1:00."

"Thanks." Miss Warner? Whoever.

But that's how I got my first job in funeral service, typing death certificates part-time. And I actually did call Mr. Bishop back the next week and went to meet him. He was rude, ignorant-acting, and crude, but he did encourage me to apply for an apprentice license and told me how to go about doing it.

About three weeks after I started working at William S. Maxwell's Funeral Home (he was deceased), I was standing around with Jackie, the only licensed funeral director in the place, the embalmer—Darian, and Darian's assistant, Donald. We did that often, hung around each other, because we were all of us under 30 years old, me being the baby at 20. We were talking and heating up hot dogs in the microwave. I had eaten about five when they noticed and began joking about my man-sized appetite. I didn't think anything of it.

CHAPTER 33

It wasn't the appetite that tipped me off, but by the first week in February I knew it was time for a home pregnancy test. The stick turned blue. I did, too.

When I told Tony, he didn't do the classic drama thing and say it wasn't his. He just asked what I was going to do. I told him I couldn't keep it. I was too young! I wasn't finished with school! I barely knew him!

"Well, I don't believe in abortion," he said.

"So what do you think we're going to do?"

"You could have the baby and then leave it with me when you go back to Indiana."

"Are you crazy? Besides, I thought you said you'd go back there with me!"

"I don't know about all that."

I stormed out of the apartment. He stormed out right after me. I know because he passed me on the highway and I was driving pretty fast. Now, where is that fool going? I wondered.

I called my mother. "I'm a little bit pregnant."

"A little bit pregnant!? What's 'a little bit pregnant?!'"

"All right—I'm pregnant."

"Tony?"

"Yeah."

"Oh, Jesus. Well? What are you going to do?"

"I can't have a baby."

"Right...well, just let me know what you do."

The short bitch knew the phone number and address of a clinic. When I made an appointment, she offered to go with me.

Tony absolutely refused. "And I'm not putting any money in your hand so you can go and kill my baby!"

"Well, stupid, you'll give it to me afterwards, and that'll be like you *paid me* to do it!"

I called Nnarami. He answered his own phone, not the sweetheart. He actually asked me to come over!

We watched TV and chit-chatted. He showed me a greeting card from someone in his family that said, "Get married soon!" Then he got serious and asked about Tony. "Does he treat you nice? Does he make candlelight dinners for you? Do you love him? Dump him."

"Why?"

"Get rid of him."

"For what?" (*Foryouforyouforyou*)

Instead, Nnarami got playful again, and tickled me into taking my clothes off. He commented on the weight I was picking up. And then he checked it out more closely...

He called the day after that.

"Will you get me a present?" he asked.

"What kind of present?"

"I need a bowtie. Black and cream."

"A bowtie, black and cream," I repeated.

"Yes."

"Sure, I guess I can do that."

"That's good stuff," he said, and I could hear him smiling!

That was enough to have me drop just about every extracurricular thing for the next week, while I hunted all over the city for just the right bowtie for Nnarami. And his favorite cologne, too, while I was at it.

CHAPTER 34

About 100 yards from the bus stop was a non-descript, 4-story tan brick building surrounded on either side and across the street by a Texaco, Pizza Hut, Blockbuster Video, Citibank, and Johnson's Funeral Home. I didn't know that this building was where we were headed as I followed Sheila. It made sense, though, unless they were doing abortions at the funeral home. They could have been. They had all the right equipment.

"Medical Professional Building" was painted in gold in very small letters on the tinted glass front doors. I thought about the number of times I had been on this block and hadn't even noticed this building. *That's a good thing*, I thought. I wondered if I would have gone in if the sign had read: ABORTION CLINIC. Probably not. But an abortion is just a medical procedure, so it made sense that they were being done in a regular doctor's office.

Inside the front doors, the entire foyer was mirrored. It was not furnished or decorated save for a couple of faux ficus trees and a pay phone. Dr. Anthony Brown's office was first on the right. The door, darkly tinted glass, was unlocked, so we walked right in. Sheila pointed me towards the receptionist's cubicle to our left and took a seat in the waiting area.

"Hi, uh... I'm Lynn Joseph? I have an appointment for, uh..."

"Yes, Lynn. Could you complete this registration form and return it to me?" the receptionist twanged sweetly. *Where did she get that country accent so close to downtown DC?* I was awash with relief that I didn't have to say much more than I did. I tried to read the name tag on the young woman's pink scrub dress, but her long, wavy brown hair covered it. Just then, she flipped the mass of hair over her shoulder. *Cynthia,* I found out, handed me a clipboard with the form and a few extra pieces of paper attached to it. I flipped through them on the way to the empty seat next to Sheila. Registration form. Explanation of procedure. What to expect. Informed Consent Form. I filled in the registration form in short order, ignored the other papers, and went back up to the window. I handed Cynthia the entire clipboard, but she gave me the other forms back.

"Keep those to read over," she said, "and a nurse will call you back shortly, okay?"

Sheila was reading an old Redbook magazine. I didn't see anything interesting scattered on the table in front of us, so I just took in my surroundings.

The chairs, in pairs with a small table separating each set, were arranged around the perimeter of the room. Another square of chairs was inside that, and then a third. Looking from above, it was a box-within-a-box configuration.

At 10:00 am, the room was half-filled with Black, White, and Hispanic women of varying ages. There were only a few pairs of vacant chairs. I hoped the people sitting next to empty seats were waiting for someone and were not there alone. Only one man, Hispanic, sat in the waiting area. Good for him! *Where were all the other guys? What were they thinking? These women were going to go through some real traumatic shit, and they, the motherfuckers who made it all possible, didn't even think it was important enough to be there. A damn shame. Sorry-asses. Tony's sorry ass.*

Nobody talked. We all just read the tattered, outdated magazines or dozed or stared blankly ahead. There was great interest for about the space of 2 seconds whenever the front door opened and someone new walked in. *Who's that? Why is she here? Who's with her? Not a guy. Her best friend? A relative? What's she wearing?*

A White woman with stringy, blonde hair, tight jeans, and a fleece jacket walked in who was visibly pregnant, at least 5 or 6 months along. *Surely she wasn't there for...naaaah.*

The door leading to the recesses of the office opened and everyone turned or looked up to see a very pretty young Black girl walk out, looking very unaffected. As she approached her companion, a Hispanic girl of about the same age, the friend stood, put on her coat, and handed the Black girl hers. The companion was looking concerned at first, her eyebrows knit close together in a sad, questioning look, but her features softened when she did not see any emotion reflected on the golden brown face in front of her. The two began whispering, the only sound to be heard in the room besides the turning of pages and the snatches of conversation coming from behind the receptionist's window. They both spoke Spanish. It was funny to hear foreign words flowing so easily from a familiar brown mouth! *Why does this Black girl speak such fluent Spanish? Did she learn it in school? Maybe she lives in an ethnically mixed neighborhood. Maybe she is ethnically mixed.* Her hair was longer than average, well past her shoulders, and maybe that wasn't a perm that was barely restraining the loose wave pattern. Both of their jeans were too tight.

The White woman who had just entered returned her forms to Cynthia and stood at the window for a moment to take a pack of cigarettes out of her jacket pocket. She tapped one out, then turned and headed for the door after she asked about how long it would be before she was called. "Gina! Come on." She had the same country twang as Cynthia, but her voice was deep, scratchy and unpleasant. I picked up a Vogue and flipped through it. So many ads. All the flaps on the perfume sample pages were open. I started to sniff anyway, until one page had a dirt smudge on it. *Euuuwww.* Lynn Joseph.

Somebody had called my name. "Huh? Oh. Here!" I said. I tossed the magazine back on the table and began gathering up my coat and papers. Sheila stretched out her arm across my chair and said, "Where do you think I'm going?" *Right*. I dropped the things back on the chair and walked double speed to the door where the nurse was standing, holding it open with her body, and followed short, stocky Jennifer with the pixie haircut on through.

Her white-stockinged legs swish-swished past some darkened business-looking offices, past a tiny, brightly lit room with a few chairs in it, around a corner, past some closed doors, and finally to an examination room.

"Take off your clothes from the waist down, get up on the table, and put that sheet over you. The doctor will be in to examine you."

Twenty minutes later when he arrived, Dr. Brown seemed to be in a big hurry, although not too unpleasant. Jennifer was right behind him. I heard her thighs.

"Hello, Miss..." He glanced back over his shoulder at the clipboard on the little counter as he pulled on a pair of latex examination gloves. Powderless. "Joseph. How are you feeling today?"

"Full."

Dr. Brown didn't laugh. I don't think he heard me. "Good. Great. I'm going to do a brief pelvic examination. We'll see what's going on...no, the metal one is fine," he finished, to Jennifer, who was indicating a choice of speculums to him. She took it over to the sink and ran some hot water on it as he pulled the stirrups out of the end of the table.

"Feet in the stirrups, please, and slide down all the way to the end of the table. A little more. More. Some more." I felt like I was falling off the table.

"That's it."

Dr. Brown adjusted the paper and plastic-backed sheet over my knees so that I couldn't see what was going on underneath. Then he swung a bright light around from the wall until it shone under the sheet. I could no longer feel the breeze from his movements, but rather the warmth from the lamp.

Jennifer handed him the speculum.

"Relax, please."

The examination was routine, swift. Dr. Brown ventured an educated guess based on the information on my clipboard and his own findings that I was eight weeks along. Afterwards, when I was dressed again, Jennifer escorted me back past the closed doors and around the corner to the brightly lit room with the three chairs, where she drew my blood. Then I trailed her back down the hall, thinking we were headed towards the waiting room. She stopped in front of one of the business offices, however, flipped on the light switch, and indicated that I should have a seat in front of the big desk.

"Now a counselor's gonna come in to get some more information and talk with you. Take care."

As Jennifer turned in the doorway to leave, she handed my clipboard to the counselor, who was walking in just then. She wore a navy blue pinstripe pantsuit with a crisp-looking white blouse. Her pearls looked antique, her dark brown hair was swept up in a french roll, her nails were short but manicured. Trish was tall, at least 5'10", maybe a little shorter without the heels she had on. Her skin looked flawless. The makeup, if she was wearing any (I couldn't tell, but I assumed she must be because she just looked so "polished," as my mom would say) was about my shade, a little lighter, maybe—"Creamed Coffee"—and was applied perfectly.

"Lynn Joseph?" she asked, reading the paper on top.

"Yes."

"Hi." She used the familiar greeting rather impersonally. Her hands were full with my clipboard, her briefcase, and some other papers, so she did not extend one to shake. She walked around and sat at the desk, dropping everything on top and then sorting through it: briefcase on the floor, stack of papers on the side, clipboard in front. I didn't have time to peruse the office before the counselor arrived, so I did it then in those two minutes. I could tell that the office didn't belong to anyone in particular. There was no ego wall, for one thing. You know, that's the wall in full view behind the desk where the doctor or other professional frames his awards and degrees. There were no family photos on the desk, no papers scattered about. A blotter, a telephone, an empty pencil holder and a lamp. The woman did not look comfortable. I forgave her for her impersonality. She wasn't being a snob. She was just new there, too.

"Lynn, my name is Trish Maguire. I'm a counselor here. The first thing I need to do is get some information from you about your medical history, so to make it easier for both of us, I'll ask the questions and fill in your answers."

After the medical history, Trish wanted to review the other papers that had been given to me in the waiting area, the ones I left in the waiting area.

"I left the papers out there. Should I go get them?"

"No, we have to do this orally, anyway. It says here that you are approximately eight weeks pregnant. Did you know that?"

"Yeah, and Dr. Brown said so in the exam."

"Do you know your options?" *Options?* I didn't come for options.

"My options?" I asked.

"Yes. You could carry the baby to term and raise it. Or there's carrying the baby to term and putting it up for adoption..."

"Oh, yes. My options. Yeah."

"Okay, then. What have you decided to do?"

"Can I just not be pregnant anymore?" I whined.

"Not without a little bit of surgery," Trish said, good-naturedly. I was glad to see the sister loosen up a little.

"I can't have a baby."

"Okay. Termination of pregnancy, then?"

I nodded.

"Are you sure?"

"Yeah, pretty sure."

"Okay, then I need to explain the entire procedure and the risks to you. If you have any questions, feel free to ask them at any time."

I scooted my chair up really close to the desk, leaned forward, and folded my arms on the edge, lacing my fingers.

"The procedure will take place in one of our exam rooms, a little larger than the one you were in today. A nurse will be present during the operation. Once you are in the stirrups, the doctor will insert a speculum into your vagina and give you a local anesthetic in the groin area."

Trish opened one of the desk drawers and pulled out a small plastic speculum and a huge needle and showed them to me. She made an inserting motion with the speculum, then demonstrated opening and locking it in place. Holding it still, she took the needle, and pretended to inject an area to the side of the speculum. Then she put them both back, closed the drawer, and opened another one. She seemed to be picking up several items.

"When the area is sufficiently numb, he will then dilate your cervix by inserting a series of dilators increasing in size." Trish showed me the items from the second drawer, one by one. All seven or so of them. They looked like Tootsie pops on long sticks that got bigger, and bigger, and bigger...

"When you are dilated to so many centimeters, depending on the period of gestation and how large the opening to your cervix already is, the doctor will insert a vacurette which suctions out the contents of the uterus." Trish put the last Tootsie pop down and made circular sweeping motions in the air with her right hand as her left hand, I supposed, pretended to hold a hose away from the imaginary disembodied pelvis on the desk between us. I pictured my grandmother preparing to stuff a Thanksgiving turkey, and it was not a delectable image.

"Finally, he will use a curette, usually a long, spoon shaped instrument...like...this one," she explained, dropping her invisible vacuum set-up and fishing in yet another drawer for the appropriate instrument, "to remove any material that might be left in the uterus." Trish was now making scraping motions with the curette. You know that feeling you get when somebody scratches their nails down a chalkboard? Yeah.

"That's it. Now, naturally, there are risks involved, as with any surgical procedure. There is the risk of infection, perforation of the uterus resulting in hysterectomy, and retained products of conception.

"Afterwards, you will rest in a recovery room for about 30 minutes, and then you will be allowed to go home. I suggest that you dress warmly and comfortably, do not eat anything after midnight the night before, and you might want to be accompanied by a friend or relative on that day. Any questions?"

I peered at Trish from behind the desk where I had sunk, my eyes barely visible above the ledge, which I held onto with a fingertip grip. "Uuuuugh," was all I could think of to say, but that didn't constitute a question, so Trish didn't answer it.

"You have with you, or rather, in the waiting area, a copy of the Informed Consent Form that you will be required to sign when you come back for your procedure."

Question. "Come back?"

"Yes, come back. We won't do the procedure today. We need time to get the results of your pelvic and your blood work back, and you could use the time to think things over. Make sure you read the Informed Consent Form in the meantime. You'll sign it when you return. So! Any more questions? About the procedure, the risks, your options, anything?"

"Uh uh."

"Okay, then. Sign this paper saying that you were counseled on all the things I just mentioned, take it to the receptionist's window, and make an appointment for a week from today, if you can. I wouldn't go much longer than that." I stood up and took the paper from her. We shook hands.

"Thanks," I told her.

"No problem," Trish said, and smiled for the first time. "You take care."

I went for the abortion a week later, on the first day of March. Sheila accompanied me again. I begged her for some of the shiny Granny Smith apple she munched on in the waiting room.

"You really shouldn't eat anything, like they said."

"I know, but I'm so hungry. A little bit won't hurt, will it?"

"I don't know, Joe. Maybe not the apple part, since it's pretty light, but definitely not the skin."

So Sheila scraped the skin off the apple with her teeth and bit off pieces for me. I made sure I chewed the apple very well.

In the examination room, finally, after a 40-minute wait, everything went pretty much as Trish had described. Dr. Brown was there, and I had a new nurse, Diane. I asked, but she wouldn't let Sheila come in the room with me. She consented to holding my hand in Sheila's place.

I put my feet into the stirrups and scooted down to the edge of the table until it felt like I would fall off. I relaxed as Dr. Brown inserted the speculum and locked it in place so that it stayed open on its own. After Diane rubbed the area with an alcohol pad, Dr. Brown used a rather large needle to inject the local anesthetic which numbed my groin area. It stung more than a little pinch, but wasn't too terrible. I suppose I was padded enough down there. Dr. Brown waited a little while, humming a little tune and fiddling with instruments around the room. Then he checked to make sure I was numb.

"Can you feel that?"

"What are you doing?" I asked. I could feel something, but wasn't sure what.

"Hand me another syringe, Diane." I got another injection, but Dr. Brown didn't wait this time. He slowly began to dilate my cervix with the dilators.

I didn't feel any pain, just pressure—pushing, twisting and pulling. It wasn't very much more uncomfortable than the pelvic exam. I had my eyes closed, doing my best to imagine other activities. Then Diane turned on a loud machine, the suction contraption, and Dr. Brown settled in to the serious job at hand. I was fine for the first few passes of the wand inside my uterus, but then it got to be a little much. Picture someone scooping and scraping out the inside of a pumpkin for Halloween. Over and over and over this went on, and I imagined that my uterus was scraped raw. I reached out my left arm for Diane. She came over and held my hand.

I wanted to squirm, scoot, shake a leg or something, but was afraid to. I didn't want to cause Dr. Brown to slip and miss. "When is he going to be finished?" I wasn't asking. I was begging.

"Where are you from?" Dr. Brown asked.

"Indiana. Why?" I whined.

"It's okay, it's okay," Diane sang.

"Oh, just asking. When was the last time you were there?"

"I don't know!" I knew what he was doing. He was trying to take my mind off the discomfort. Arrgggh! Well, I had nothing better to do, so I decided to give it a try. "A few months ago. Christmas."

"You like it there?" he asked, but the jig was up already.

"When are you going to be finished?"

"Okay, okay," Diane whispered, patting my hand, the one that was squeezing hers.

"Oh, it'll be over in no time," Dr. Brown said. "Just keep talking. Diane? Curette, please. You're doing fine. This doesn't hurt at all!" Diane left my side to get the instrument.

"Noooo, pleeeease! It's so uncomfortable! Can't you stop scraping?"

"I have to make sure I do a good job, otherwise, you'll have to come back and go through this again. You could get very sick."

"Okay, just hurry!" I whispered. Tears were streaming down the sides of my face, into my ears. I had helped them get there by shaking my head from side to side, the only movement I felt I could safely make.

Suddenly my chest began to heave, and I got a strange, sour, acidic taste in my mouth. "I'm going to throw up!"

Diane was back at my side, and reaching down, opened a drawer on the table and pulled out a shallow, yellow plastic tray. Her movements were as smooth and calm as if she were going to be putting it there anyway, as she slid the tray in place next to my face just in time. I turned my head to the left and threw up a clear, amber-colored liquid with a few little chunks of something white in it. The apple. Apple juice.

"Miss Joseph? Dr. Brown said.

"Whaaat?" I sniffed, as Diane wiped my mouth with a paper towel.

"That's it. We're finished."

Even after my 30 minutes in recovery and a soothing cup of ginger ale, I was in no shape to get on the bus to go home. I had alternating chills and hot flashes, and I didn't feel up to a bumpy ride. I used the pay phone in the hallway outside Dr. Brown's office to call Darian at the funeral home.

"I'm at the clinic," I whispered, cold and exhausted. "Can you—"

"I'll be right there," she said.

Sheila and I sat on the air conditioning/heating unit inside the foyer and watched people come and go for about 20 minutes. Then we walked outside to wait for Darian.

A car pulled up right in front of the Medical Professional Building and parked. A woman got out and came around to the passenger side to open the door for her young companion.

"No!" the girl said. We could hear her through the closed window.

"Open the door, girl!" the woman said, exasperated.

"No! I can't go in there!"

"Open this door. You're going!" She stood there, frowning, tapping one foot on the pavement, hand on her hips, waiting. Then her expression softened. "Come on, baby. It's okay. It'll be all right. Come on, now," she coaxed, sly as a fox.

It seemed to work. The girl unlocked the door, opened it, and stood up. The woman reached around her and pressed the lock, but when she tried to shut the door, the girl didn't move and her legs seemed to give out. She slumped backwards into the front seat.

"Please, no. I can't go in there!" she begged.

The woman kept up with her winning tactic. Taking the girl by one arm, she pulled her to her feet, away from the car, and kicked the door shut. They walked slowly the 5 or so paces from the curb to the door of the building with the woman half carrying the girl. She didn't look any older than 12.

Before they got inside, Darian pulled up—in one of the hearses.

"I can't sneak out in my *own car*!" she explained upon seeing the look on my face.

"Should I just stretch out in back?" I managed a chuckle.

"Naw. We can all three fit up front. It's not like we're going far. You're going home, right?"

Darian dropped Sheila and me off at 3rd street, apologizing for the bumps she hit on the way. "Call me if you need anything!"

Tony didn't call or return any of my calls for a week. Then he came by to drop off half of the money and a big, child-sized teddy bear.

"Thanks a lot for nothing, really," I spat at him.

We argued and made right up. He seemed hurt about the baby, but said that he came by because he missed me and needed to be close to me right then.

We named the bear Kenji, and eventually bought him a wardrobe of little T-shirts to wear. He even had a godfather, a man who worked at the funeral home with Tony. I let Tony have "custody" of Kenji because I didn't have much space in my room at the Rho house.

The day after my two-week check up found me back at Rami's place again. "Did you dump that guy yet?"

"No." I thought about how nice Tony had been for those past two weeks. He even played hide-and-go-seek with me!

"Why not?"

I was quiet for a minute. There was something on the news about bombing abortion clinics or something. I told Nnarami to watch that for a second. He looked at the TV and then caught on.

"Does that have something to do with you?" I nodded.

"Are you pregnant?"

I shook my head. "No."

"But you were."

"Yes," I nodded.

"You had an abortion?"

For the first time it was I who didn't answer. My underarms began to sting when I realized I hadn't thought this thing through. I hadn't considered what he might think of me, allowing myself to get pregnant, then having an abortion. I covered my mouth with one hand and turned my head to look out the window—well, *at* the window because I wasn't really looking to see anything, especially the expression on Rami's face.

"You were pregnant the last time you were here," he said quietly, and not particularly to me.

Nnarami stepped over and joined me on the papasan. Sitting behind me, he wrapped his arms and legs around me and held me tightly. We sat that way for a long time as he stroked my hair. I let my head fall back onto his shoulder and he kissed my neck, the side of my face, then turned me around to kiss my lips. Later he made a tender, sweet kind of love to me, different from the play- or passion-filled sessions before.

Then Rami got up and rooted around in his closet for a minute. When he emerged, he was putting on the T-shirt I'd hand-painted for him the summer before.

"See? I still have it."

I smiled weakly at Rami and got up to get dressed. I was supposed to feel good about that, and I did, a little. Except the shirt had been hidden away. I thought about the sweetheart. I thought about Tony. I thought about Rami and me, about how much I wanted us to be together, but realizing that we had both made other beds and lain in them. Why did it take such a drastic situation on my part for Rami to be as tender as he had been in the beginning?

"I don't think we should do this anymore," I said. I figured it was the right thing to say, but

(Pleasepleaseplease disagree with me before I walk out this door!)

"Okay."

I drove home easily drowning out the radio, and the next day, Tony was delighted to receive a new bottle of cologne…just out of the blue.

CHAPTER 35

I hardly lived at the Rho house anymore, and barely knew what was going on there. Both Irene and Sheila had relatively steady boyfriends who were in frequent attendance at the house, so there wasn't much of the brothel-like activity going on anymore. Robert and Jamie were frequent guests even though I wasn't there; DC was a great get-away for the military boys, and the Rho house was the perfect place to stay. They even brought other schoolmates along. A.J. moved out, and I never even found out the reason why. Apparently, though, he fell out with either Irene or Sheila. A guy named Burt had moved into the basement. So it was Sheila, Irene, Natalie, Burt, several visitors, and sometimes me, living together in the house on Third Street.

One night, Ray had a guest named Shannon staying over at his and Tony's place. She and I got along pretty well; at least this one was *of age*. Ray had had some girls sleep over who looked likely to land him in jail. Once I bumped into one of them coming out of the bathroom.

"Off to work?" I asked, fishing. She looked all of 12 years old.

"Naw."

"*School?*"

"Naw, I'm outta school!"

"Umm. Where'd you go?"

" I went to Bowie." *Whew!*

"Oh! Bowie State (University)?"

"Naw. Bowie *High*. You got a tampon or something?"

175

Euwww! Anyhow…the next morning, Ray and Tony went to work, but I was off and so was Shannon. We had no idea what to do to entertain ourselves.

"Let's watch a movie," she suggested.

As I hooked up Tony's VCR to the TV, Shannon's girlfriend showed up, and the three of us contemplated which movie we'd watch from the guys' scanty collection of about 8 tapes.

"Well, there's a tape in the machine. What's that?" asked the friend.

"I don't know," I said as I pushed it in.

The screen lit up in vivid flesh tones with a close-up of Tony's hands on some girl's ass. She was straddling him, and he was smiling and talking to somebody else in the room over her shoulder. I pushed the stop button quickly.

"Noooo! What was that?" Shannon yelled.

"You know what it is," I said, "and we don't need to be watching it."

"Oh, no!" Shannon said. "I want to see if Ray's in it!" The friend's eyes were as big as saucers. She looked stunned. I *was* stunned. I wanted them to leave.

Shannon pushed play and we watched the tape. First Tony screwed that girl with her on top. Then Ray joined them and they screwed her at the same time. Ray left, and Tony screwed her on the edge of the bed. I pushed fast forward to hurry this thing up, but that only made it look worse. The scene changed. Another girl was sucking Tony's dick. Another scene. A girl, this one decent-looking, squirming all over the bed. Tony and Ray taking turns fingering her. Then Ray screwed her. All the while there were two other guys in the room who walk past the scene at least once. Then Tony was on the screen saying that it was November 25th, but not what year. I looked to see if I could recognize the location. I knew all of the furnishings; they were the same ones that Tony had now. Same bedspread and sheets, bedside table, lamp...but the room did look a little different.

"Girl, I hope y'all using something," the friend said as we rewound the tape back to where it started. "Come on, Shannon, let's get out of here. Lynn, what you gon' do, girl? You need a ride somewhere?"

"No, I have a car. I'll be leaving soon."

They left. Ray stopped by about 30 minutes after that. I just sat on Tony's bed and waited for him to leave before taking the last of my things out to my car and speeding home.
When I got there, I told everybody in the house what happened. Of course they were shocked and outraged! I called my mother, I called Bill's wife...everybody I could think of, and told them about the Porno King. When I holler, I holler loud!

"Thank God you didn't have that baby by him. It might have been born with horns! Or something."

Exhausted, I decided to take a nap and then start out driving to Indiana to take a break. Robert and Jamie were at the house. "Is there anything I can do for you?" Jamie asked, with his sweet self.

"No, I'll be okay. Just wake me up in about 5 hours, okay?"

Tony stopped by the house while I was asleep, but somebody's boyfriend wouldn't let him in, so he called.

"I'm sorry," he said. "I know what you saw."

Damn! I had forgotten to unhook the VCR.

"What are you talking about? I haven't seen anything. But I don't want to talk right now."

"Stop lying, Lynn. I know you saw that tape. But I swear it was before I met you."

I didn't say anything.

"I swear! I'm not lying. I talked to my dad about it, and I burned the tape."

"You did?"

"Yeah."

"Tony, that shit was NASTY! It was SICK! How could you DO something like that?"

"I don't know," he whined. "I was hurt at the time...this girl...I hated women. I know I shouldna done it. But I told you, the tape is gone. I burned it."

"So?"

"Are you coming back?"

"I don't know. I don't think so, Tony. Everything will just remind me—"

"The tape wasn't made here. I was living somewhere else. I TOLD you that was before I met you!"

"But the furniture is the same. I'm having a real problem with that furniture."

"Stop being stupid!"

I got angry then. "Look, I don't want to talk to your nasty ass! Don't call me anymore!"

"Lynn—" he started, but I hung up the phone, unplugged it and tried to nap. That wasn't happening, so I was still exhausted when Jamie knocked on my door, peeked in, and told me it was time for me to get up to go.

"Jamie, I'm so tired! Maybe I shouldn't try to drive to Indiana. Maybe I should just go somewhere closer, like Baltimore." Jamie just nodded in agreement.

"No, I don't even feel like going there. I shouldn't let that boy run me away because of something *he* did, should I?"

Jamie shook his head, then walked completely into the room. He held one hand up to me (I was in the loft). I took it and he squeezed it reassuringly.

"Let me know if you need anything," he said.

"Wait a second," I said. I let go of his hand and climbed down from the loft. Jamie reached out to hug me, and though we had never even touched before, I went into his arms and he held me as I cried for a minute. Then he kissed me a few times on my forehead and cheeks, and wiped my tears away by nuzzling his face against mine. Until then, I had only looked at Jamie as

Robert's friend, but I began to see him in a whole new light that evening.

That weekend Robert and Jamie were in town again, and they went with us to a party that the bro's were throwing at the frat house. We figured Nnarami would be there with his sweetheart, so my sorors dressed me up really feminine and sexy. Jamie hardly left my side all night, and Nnarami ate his heart out. He tried to talk to me when we found ourselves alone on the back porch for a minute.

"Did you dump your boyfriend? Is that the new guy you're with?" he asked flippantly.

"Where's your little sweetheart?" I hadn't seen Assette all evening. And then people started coming out onto the porch saying "Ooh! Sorry!" because they thought they were busting up a little tryst. They were!

"No, it's okay," we said. We stood there just staring at each other until the porch got crowded, and we both found ourselves talking to other people.

Jamie danced with me all night. I don't think I got a chance to dance with anyone else. Turned out, he was a pretty sexy dancer! We went home and he slept in my room from then on instead of on the sofabed.

At first I was disappointed that he wasn't as well endowed as I imagined he would be. Heck—as I was *used to* guys being! Jamie had what looked like a mushroom.

Turns out, a mushroom is a VERY useful tool! Virtually all of the vagina's nerve endings are concentrated at the entrance, making that area highly sensitive. Since a mushroom doesn't go much further than the entrance, it keeps hitting... all... those...

all of those ...thousands...
and thousands...*ahhh*...
of sense—*ummm*...
of sensitive...*oooh*...

nerves…nerves—
right there…
right *there*…

"JAMIIIIEEE!"

Tony called the next weekend, Sunday morning. He had been treading lightly since the sex, lies, and videotape. It was Easter, and Jamie was not in town. I was getting ready to go to church, so I got off the phone quickly. Guess who showed up at the service?

Tony found a seat next to me. I had put my sweater and purse on the pew between me and the next person, taking up a whole seat, which Tony was then able to occupy. That's what I get for acting ugly up in the church!

I kept waiting for God to strike him down, but it didn't look like that was going to happen. I figured I would help Him out a bit.

I got real busy with my pocket-sized concordance, looking stuff up, and tearing off pieces of my program to mark specific places in my Bible. Then I shoved the book at Tony and had him read each scripture in order, in rapid succession, so that he would get my point:

1) (Ecclesiastes 10:5)
"There is an evil which I have seen…"

2) (Jeremiah 21:12)
"…because of the evil of your doings."

3) (Ezekiel 33:11)
"Turn ye, turn ye from your evil ways."

4) (1 Thessalonians 5:22)
"Abstain from all appearance of evil."

5)   (Ezekiel 3:19)
"Yet if thou warn the wicked, and he turn not from his wickedness, nor from his wicked way, he shall die…"

6)   (Proverbs 17:11)
"An evil man seeketh only rebellion: therefore a cruel messenger shall be sent against him."

I was smug den a mongfecky! I had *God* cosigning on my righteous indignation!

Tony sat with the bible open on his lap for a while after he read the last scripture, while I continued to enjoy the service.

Finally he gave the bible back to me. I started to close it, but he put his hand in the way and held it open. Then he pointed to a scripture on the same page as my last one:

(Proverbs 17:9)
"He that covereth a transgression seeketh love."

Ah, shit!

Awwww…

Tony called me as soon as he made it home from church. "Will you go for a ride with me? I really want to see you."

"You just saw me."

"I know. I want to spend some time with you."

"Fine. Come get me."

Tony and Kenji (strapped in the back seat) picked me up and we went driving aimlessly around town (which seemed to be their only purpose) with the Camaro Cruise Club. There were about eight Camaros in all, drivers and their women just out for a Sunday ride. Tony seemed to be enjoying himself, though, as the ghetto motorcade attracted lots of attention. That was Tony!

Anything with flash—cars, clothes, an unusual occupation—that was bound to attract attention was the thing for him! I was bored near 'bout to death!

Afterwards, Tony took me to dinner at my favorite Chinese restaurant. Over dinner he told me how much he missed me and said that he was getting hard just looking at me. I covered Kenji's ears. Not far from the restaurant, I saw a playground, and I wanted to stop and play. We put Kenji on the sliding board, and I got on the swings.

"I can't stand being this close to you and can't make love to you," Tony said as he felt me up, calling himself pushing me.

We left the playground, and ended up outside Tony's apartment.

"I need to get something," he announced. I just sat in the car with the bear.

"Come on, Lynn."

"I'm not going in that apartment."

"It wasn't this apartment!"

"Fine," I said, getting out of the car. He was starting to ruin what had been a mindless, but enjoyable evening.

I sat Kenji at the dining table and stood in Tony's bedroom doorway with a disgusted look on my face.

"Stop looking like that. Come here and sit next to me."

"Maybe when you get some new furniture."

"It's new sheets! Look!" he said, throwing back the comforter in a huff. The sheets did look different from the ones in the video. I went over and gingerly perched on the front edge of the bed.

"What?"

"Come here, baby…" he murmured, leaning over to kiss me. My armpits began to tingle.

"Stop it!" I jumped up off the bed. "I thought you came to get something. Get it, and let's go!"

"Why can't I make love to you?"

"I'm not ready yet."

"It's been two weeks!" For Tony, two weeks without sex was like...*uh-uh*. Nope!

"So you're gonna put a time limit on it? I may never get over that shit I saw! I might have to be hypnotized so I can forget about it!"

"Naw, naw, Lynn. I *know* you! You can't go more than a couple of weeks without sex. Who you fucking? Your ex-boyfriend? One of them military boys? I know they be hanging out at your house."

"No."

"Well, then what is it? How you gon' have a man and not make love to him? Something's wrong with that."

"I told you I'm not ready!"

"Naw, man, naw. Come on, baby. I want you so bad right now. I've been good, I did everything you asked me to do. I burned the tape, I haven't bothered you, I changed the sheets, even went to church... I been trying to show you I've changed. I'm not the same guy who made that tape. Baby, please." He came over to me and tried to touch me.

"No."

"Why?"

"I just don't feel like it." I twisted away from him, but walked further into his room. I was standing on the other side of the bed, by the window. I was trapped. Tony climbed across the bed.

"That's a lie! I know you do! Look! Your nipples are hard—" (he swept his hand across them and I smacked it away) "your panties are probably already wet—" (he put a hand between my legs, and I slapped him and ran to the other side of the room).

"Leave me alone!"

"Why?"

"I love Jamie!"

Oops! Tony had been on his knees on the bed, but this information made him sit down correctly on the edge. Then he got up, opened the window, and took a deep breath while I stood on the other side of the bed with my hand over my mouth.

"I don't believe this. You're fucking the military boy."

"No."

"Don't—don't lie to me! It makes perfect sense. Why else wouldn't you sleep with your own man?"

"I'm just trying to be fair. Until I sort this out, I can't sleep with him, so I shouldn't sleep with you either."

"Bullshit, Lynn."

"Tony—"

Tony sat back down on the edge of the bed with his back to me. His shoulders heaved up and down once heavily, and then uncontrollably. He was crying.

I only expected to see Jamie sporadically on weekends, the way I *had* been seeing him, but things had changed. A couple of times, Jamie showed up at the house in the middle of the week. My sorors would call me at Tony's with some excuse for me to come home. Usually the Short Bitch pretended to be sick (she *was* sickly), and I was needed to take her to the doctor, the hospital, her sister's house…wherever. Tony didn't seem to suspect anything, and Jamie never complained.

Perhaps, maybe even only once, he should have.

CHAPTER 36

My 21st birthday was near. I planned exactly what I wanted to do, so on that day, everything was in order.

That morning, I got up and went to work at the funeral home. I had asked to just embalm all day, but there were no bodies to be done.

The staff threw me a surprise party. They sprang for lunch and had cake and ice cream. The cake said:

ALL-IN-ONE-DAY, TUESDAY
Lynn!

which jokingly promised that the way the industry treats us (overworking and underpaying), the best I'd be able to do would be to have a brief, state-funded, combination wake and funeral on a bad day.

After work, Darian put on a chauffeur's hat and we picked up the rest of the party girls in one of Maxwell's limos: Carla, Irene, Sheila, a Maxwell's secretary (Marsha, who was off that day), and Pat—whose husband worked with us.

We went to Pizza Hut because I wanted to "eat pizza naked in a limousine." But we dined in because nobody was going to be bold enough to strip down to their undies in the car.

Next we went to the movies. "Wild Orchid" was playing, and we heard it was supposed to have been rated X at one time, but was now rated NR. We giggled and decided to go see it.

Then we hit a bar. I had to ask the bouncer to check my ID. He did, and told me happy birthday! I had one drink, flirted with a couple of guys, and we left. We drove around town for hours. I think the other ladies were looking for something to do.

Not me; I fell asleep, bumped my head on the window, said "Owww," and went back to sleep.

At around 5:00 am, Darian pulled into Tony's apartment complex's parking lot. Another limo pulled up behind us and Tony got out.

"Where have you been?" I asked.

"Out. You're not the only one who can stay out all night," he said.

"But it's *my birthday*! Yours was three months ago!" I reminded him (which made him a black, male, February Pisces, and they're all alike—let that be a warning to you!).

I saw I couldn't have anything to myself without him coming along and robbing my joy.

Jamie asked me to go to the big dance with him at the military college, the same one I'd gone to with Robert the year before. My brother Bill had attended VMC, and that dance was where he'd proposed to his wife. A lot of girls get engaged that night, I'd heard. Can I tell you how excited I was?

So I got beautiful in a black and gold strapless dress that matched his uniform. The bitches took pictures and fed me birth control pills as if I needed extra protection for this one enchanted evening.

Since VMC's graduation was the following weekend, Jamie's entire family flew up from Washington State, and they went to the dance, too. We all liked each other pretty well, and they called Jamie's and my pictures "pre-wedding" pictures. After the dance, Jamie went home with his family for the month until he had to report to flight school.

It *was* a magical night, but Jamie didn't propose to me. I don't suppose it would have been appropriate, seeing as I had a boyfriend, and all.

CHAPTER 37

The bro's had a cookout. My sorors got me very cute again and we went. Nnarami was there. I just stared at him. And stared. And stared. I couldn't get over how good he looked! That, and how the outline of a certain part of his anatomy could be clearly seen through the bike shorts he was wearing.

Irene came over to me and whispered, "Rami said to tell you that you can look, but don't be so obvious."

I flirted outrageously with his frat brothers. Derrick and I pretended to make a music video when a slow song was on the radio. We stood really close, held hands, and looked into each other's eyes. Then we looked away. Sheila told me, "Rami's jealous. He said that's enough."

"Why can't he talk to me himself?"

On the way out the door when the party was over, Rami said goodbye to Irene and Sheila and then gave me this huge bear hug, picking me up off the ground.

"Stop it, Rami! That hurts!" Sheila and Irene kept walking away.

He put me down, but still held onto me. Armpits tingling…but oh, the thrill! I kept my arms wrapped around him, too. And then I took a very big chance.

"I am *so* in love with you."

"Oh yeah? That's good stuff!" he said with that special smile! And then: "So why aren't you with me?"

"Because you didn't want me!"

"Did I tell you that?" he asked. *Hadn't he?* But apparently the correct answer was "no".

"No. But what about your sweetheart?"

"She doesn't have anything to do with this."

"*Okay...*" I thought he would give me a clue about what I should do or say next, but he didn't.

"Well, then, I love you. Can we—"

"Shh! Don't." And then he kissed me.

I could have stayed there that way forever! Angels were siiing-ing and all that...but I really needed to know what he meant.

"Don't what? Tell you how I feel?"

"Don't love me." He moved to kiss me again, but I pulled back.

"Why not?" I whined, armpits getting hot.

"I could tell you, but then I'd have to kill you."

"So tell me and kill me quick," I responded, automatically. I remembered us having that same exchange of words the summer before, and I got choked up. "Shit!"

"Lynn! Wait a minute...listen..."

"Just forget it, Rami! Leave me alone!" I put my hands between us on his chest and tried to push away from him, but he held on tight. "Let go of me!" I knew I would start bawling if I didn't get away from him soon, and I didn't want him to see that. I cry ugly.

"Lynn, I *do* love you. I just..." but I was gone! The rest of what Rami said was lost in the wind as I broke free and ran, crying, to catch up with my friends.

Irene, Sheila and I rang Nnarami's phone a week later on his birthday. When the answering machine picked up, everybody left a birthday message—except for me. I couldn't bring myself to say anything after being prompted by his sweetheart's voice.

CHAPTER 38

Meanwhile, Sheila and Irene had discovered how expensive it was to heat a three-story row house, and the winter heating bills still hadn't been paid. The gas and then the electricity got turned off, and everyone planned to move out of the house. I wasn't working much—they had cut back my hours at Maxwell's—, so I was pissed that this happened right when I couldn't afford to move anywhere.

I came home one day from the funeral home to find that my key didn't work. I rang the bell angrily, and Irene and Sheila both came to the door.

"Go look in your room and let us know what's missing," Irene said.

"What did you bitches kidnap this time?" I asked.

A few weeks earlier when my sorors were up to some of their childish games, they kidnapped my Sigma Barbie doll and held her for $10,000 ransom. Of course I was *pissed* because they were messing with my *stuff*, but as soon as I left them alone about it, they returned her safe and sound. (Or maybe it was the sight of Sheila's favorite stuffed animal—bound and gagged, and hanging from her bedroom chandelier—that made them stop playing their silly little game. All of Irene's stuffed animals were sitting in a circle on the floor below Sheila's swinging teddy bear, with little conversation balloons taped to their faces that said things like, "Damn! He must have done some fucked up shit!")

"No joke this time. Go on up and take a look."

I raced up the stairs and into my room. At first glance I didn't notice anything because I really didn't have much there.

Then I looked at my desk under the loft. *Aw, man!* My radio was gone with Alexander O'Neil (*"Never knew love like this!"*) in the tape deck. And on the floor behind my door sat a little straw hat that used to cover the spout of one of those huge water bottles, into which I dumped all my loose change—my "goddaughter's trust fund." Everybody in the house contributed to it, and lately we had taken to putting five- and ten-dollar bills in there. *Shit!*

Irene and Sheila were in the doorway.

"My radio and my goddaughter's trust fund," I told them.

"That's all we saw, too, but we wanted you to check and make sure."

"How did they get in? When did this happen? What else is missing?"

"Well, it wasn't a forced entry. They had a key. And it must have been sometime this morning right after we all left for work. All the TVs are gone, stereos, the microwave, money, my leather jacket, jewelry…"

"Man. What about Burt and Natalie?"

"Burt's missing some of his new tools, but nothing, apparently, is missing from Natalie's room. She came by earlier, said nothing of hers was gone, and started moving her things out."

"Wait a second! All that leather and jewelry, and nothing's missing?"

"That's what *we* said. We were just figuring out what to do about it."

"We think she gave her crackhead sister the key and told her exactly what to come in and take. I guess they figured it was a good time since everybody was getting ready to move out."

"That makes sense, but oh, no—she can't get away with this!"

"We gon' beat her ass down!" Irene said.

I was already in her room, looking around. Most of her things were gone, but we lucked up when we found a brand new CD player.

"Come on," I said to Irene and Sheila. We went to the basement, took the CD player out of its box and smashed it on the concrete floor. (This was back when CD's were first coming out, and I guess we weren't convinced this new medium would take off, or we probably shoulda kept it, huh?) Back upstairs, we proceeded to trash the rest of Natalie's belongings.

When Natalie arrived later that evening to gather more of her stuff, she couldn't get in either, since the locks were changed. She bitched and cursed and threatened us for about 20 minutes before she left. When she got wherever she was going, she called Sheila and threatened some more. Sheila was cool, though, and told Natalie that she was welcome to come and get her things—with a police escort. So what time should we expect her?

Everybody was home by 4:00 pm the next day, waiting for Natalie to return. Sheila called one of the officers who took the burglary report to let him know that the culprit had arrived. Officer Randolph arrived 15 minutes later, and we let the madwoman and her cousin in the house.

Boy, was she upset when she discovered all the havoc we had wreaked in her room! At first it looked normal, but her cousin smelled something funny as she walked down the stairs with an armful of clothes. She stuck her nose into the pile, then separated the items in half and got a look at the other side of a black dress.

"Nat! Giiiirl, them bitches bleached your shit!"

Natalie came running out to the top of the stairs. "What?!" she shrieked, and ran back into her room to check the rest of her clothes.

She came downstairs with an armful of the ruined wardrobe a couple of minutes later. "That's okay, mothafuckas. I'mmo get y'all's asses!" Her cousin had the same message for us on her way back in.

"Did they fuck up *all* your shit?"

"Yeah, girl. Them bitches! And they cut up my mattress, too."

We just stood on the porch with Officer Randolph until they finished.

"Make sure you get all of it because you're not getting back in," Irene said to Natalie on one of her trips.

"Hey, none of that," warned Officer Randolph. "Let her get her things quietly."

"Yeah, bitch," Natalie spat. She jumped at Irene, who didn't even flinch; Natalie was as tiny as Sheila.

"That goes for you, too," Irene replied.

Natalie's cousin stuck her tongue out at us. We had to laugh at that. And when they were finished and had gone, we laughed again.

I knew we'd have trouble with locals.

Sheila and Irene moved out at the beginning of July. A.J. came by at the end of that week to help me disassemble the loft. It was a bad day. I bitched and moaned the entire afternoon:

Their *fathers* were paying their rent for them…
So how come they couldn't pay the *utilities*?…
That's how they could go *shopping* all the time…
They just didn't give a *shit* about anybody else…
We spent all that *money* fixing up this house…
It's a *good thing* I didn't nail this bitch to the *wall*…
Letting *thugs* move in to rob us blind…
Look—no, you can't 'cause we ain't got no *lights*…
No gas, can't *cook*…
Can't even hardly wash *my ass* in this cold water…

By then I was sitting in a tub of cold water in the dark, gingerly trying to bathe as A.J. sat on the closed toilet seat and listened to me.

"I shouldn't be going through this," I cried. "Why me?"

"It's not your fault."

"You're right. Women!"

Jamie had gone home with his family after graduation, but he stopped back through DC to see me on his way to Florida and flight school. I had three days left in the house, and he had two days before he was due in Florida. I thought he was crazy, but he insisted on staying with me in the condemned building, eating fast food, taking cold showers, and entertaining each other by candlelight after sundown. He helped me pack my personal belongings into my car.

"Are you going to be okay?" he asked when it was time for him to go. "I worry about you."

"I'll be just fine!"

"Where will you go?" he asked hesitantly. I'm sure he knew just as well as I did where I'd end up.

I told him to write me at my brother's address.

CHAPTER 39

The next day, the day after Jamie left and the last day of the month, Tony came to help me move the last of my things out of the house and into his and Ray's apartment. Spying the candles all around, he jumped to conclusions.

"You and that nigga been up in here burning candles. You were fucking him!"

"What do candles have to do with anything? There's no *electricity*—I was burning the candles for *light,* dumb-ass! Uh, are you going to move my stuff, or what?"

So then I was officially (because I had no place else to go) unofficially (because I was not on the lease) living with Tony. We fought all the time. The women calling the apartment was the biggest thing:

—

"Can you tell Tony that Renee called?"

"Sure. Hi, Renee."

"Hey…you know what? Who are you?"

"Lynn. Tony's girlfriend."

"His girlfriend, huh?"

"Yep."

"He said you was just his "little mortician buddy.""

"He did, did he?"

"Yeah."

"Well, no, I'm his girlfriend. I live here."

"Oh, so that's *your* stuff over on the side of the bed, by that box?"

"You mean to tell me you've been here and saw my *panties* and didn't think anything of it?"

—

"Lynn, I'mmo be straight and ask you what is up."

"What you mean, Robin?"

"Are y'all together, or what? 'Cause I didn't have nothin' better to do, and I was gon' mess with him again. He said y'all weren't together."

"Oh, yeah? Well, no. We are together. I live here."

—

"This is the AT&T operator. Will you accept a collect call from Michelle?"

—

Rrrrring! Rrrrring!

"Hello?"

Click!

*6-9.

"Hello. You've just reached Yvette. I can't come to the phone right now, so please leave a message at the sound of the tone."

—

"Hello?"

"May I speak with Tony?"

"May I tell him who's calling, please?"

"Bitch!"

—

It wasn't long before one morning I suddenly announced to Tony that I was moving back out—that evening. He called me from the road on his way home from work.

"Don't go anywhere until I get there!"

Tony rushed into the apartment, to find me sitting in his room, waiting to leave.

"What do you have to say?" I asked.

He showed me a small jeweler's box and then opened it.

"Don't go," he said.

I looked at the diamond ring inside. It was simple and pretty—just what I would have wanted. I smiled.

"Tony? No, thank you. I've got to go."
He was pissed.
"Oh! All right then! Leave!"
"I will!" I said, and stormed out.

I had been in Baltimore for about a week (catching up on reading all of his cards and letters) when Jamie visited. He wanted me to come to Florida to be near him in flight school. I checked out some mortuary schools in that area and found one in Mobile, Alabama. We looked on a mileage chart and were delighted to see that it was only 50 miles from him! I sent for an application, and Jamie went back to flight school...sooo far away...

It was the last time I would ever see him.

That next week, Operation Desert Shield turned into Desert Storm. It took precedence in the news from then on, so nobody noticed the small blurbs about the first stirrings of civil unrest in Somalia.

CHAPTER 40

I was at work at Maxwell's. I got a call from A.J., whom I hadn't talked to in a while, and lots of calls from my sorors, including The Crew.

Call #1:

"Lynn, when are you leaving work? You need a ride home?"

"Nooo…I'm staying all the way in Baltimore now, but I have a car, remember?"

Call #2:

"Lynn. How are you doing? Are you okay?"

"Darlene? What are you doing calling me?"

"I was just concerned that I haven't talked to you for a while."

"Oh! That's real nice."

Call #3:

"Lynn—I need to talk to you. Can you come over right away? When do you get off work?"

"Wow! Is something wrong? What's the matter?"

"I just really need to talk to you."

"Okay, well, I'll see what I can do."

Call #4:

"Hey."

"Hey, A.J. What's up?"

"Whatcha doin'?"

"Taking a lot of calls from my sorors. I think they're up to something," I said, smiling as I tried to imagine the latest hare-brained scheme they might have concocted.

"You read the paper today?"

"Man, you know all I have time for is the obituaries! What's in it? Something interesting?"

"Same old stuff. Go talk to your sorors. I'll catch you later."

Call #5:

"Hi, Lynn. How's it going?

"Fine. Long time, no hear."

I was flattered by all the attention, but what was up? Well, apparently no one told Derrick.

Call #6:

"Hey, Joe. It's Derrick."

"Derrick! *Heeey*! It's my favorite sands! Whatcha doing calling me all the way from California?"

"I've got bad news…"

My underarms started stinging. So A.J. and my sorors knew whatever it was that Derrick knew. They were trying to protect me from something, but I was about to hear it!

"What is it, Derrick?" I felt queasy, like I would throw up.

"Are you sitting down?" he asked.

"Yes," I lied. Then I felt weak in my knees and really did need to sit down at my desk. "Yes," I said again, sitting. "What is it?"

"Nnarami was murdered."

I dropped the phone, snatched my keys off the desk, and ran upstairs and outside to my car. There I fumbled with the door, but managed to open it and fall inside. I had to get home—all the way to Baltimore, damn!

Darian and Donald ran out to the parking lot where I was trying to figure out how to get the car started. I couldn't see. My face and hands were streaked with tears and snot. I pulled my hair, beat the steering wheel with my keys...

Donald bravely reached in and pulled me kicking and flailing out of the car and carried me back inside the funeral home, into the garage where I wouldn't disturb anybody. For a second, I had a clear thought—if I couldn't act a fool in a *funeral home* because somebody had died, then what was the point?

"Derrick, nooo! Why'd you have to tell me?!" I cried into the phone in the garage. He had held on all that time, about 10 minutes, to make sure I was okay.

"I'm sorry, Joe. I thought when you heard, it should come from me. Are you okay?"

"No. What happened, D-Derrick?" My voice cracked as I teared up again.

"Well, it's been pretty hard to get any information, so none of this is confirmed yet. Anyway, Rami insisted on going to Somalia to see his mom even though some messed up political bullshit was going on. Turns out, her husband is one of the chief warlords behind it. Rami wanted to leave when things started getting bad last week, but when I talked to him, he said he couldn't get a flight out. Meanwhile, this other faction decided to try to kill Rami's stepfather. When they invaded the house, the guy wasn't there so they shot Rami instead.

"Like I said, though, none of this is confirmed. The bro's are trying to get some more information now."

"Derrick? Let me call you baaaack..."

"Okay, Joe. Take it easy. I love you."

Darian took the phone away from me and disconnected the line. Then she called Tony. It had been almost two weeks since I'd talked to him, which was since I had moved to Baltimore.

"What's going on? What's the matter?"

"Nnarami died."

"Oh. I'm sorry to hear that. Why aren't you at the morgue?" But I detected a bit of smugness in his voice, which pissed me off. That's why I snapped at him.

"Because he's in Africa, stupid!"

"Oh."

"Listen, they won't let me drive myself home. Can you come and get me?"

"Depends on where you going—to Baltimore, or with me?"

"I don't have time for that! Just come get me!"

In the meantime, I called Irene and Sheila back on conference call to let them know that I had heard the news, and that I was okay.

"Derrick said nobody was really sure, though."

"Yeah, everybody's been trying to get some confirmation that it was really Rami who was killed. It could have been anybody in the house."

"How are we supposed to find out?"

"Somebody would have to identify his body."

"Du-uh! Let's call the morgue!"

I pulled out Maxwell's copy of *The American Blue Book of Funeral Directors* and flipped through the back pages of newspapers, transportation companies, and international numbers, where I found only a listing for the U.S. Embassy in Mogadishu, Somalia.

I gave Sheila the number so that she could use her three-way to call, and after only two tries, we got a faint, static-y connection.

"I'm calling from the United States, trying to confirm a death that was reported to have happened yesterday—"

"From the United States?"

"Yes."

"Just a minute, please."

"Hello?" Another person took over the call.

"I'm calling from the United States, looking for someone, an American, who was reported dead there."

"What is the name?"

"Nnarami Obawani."

"Wait a minute, please."

"Maybe this wasn't a good idea," Irene said. "How are we going to identify him? If it's that bad over there, there's probably over a hundred people…"

"Hello?" The man was back.

"Yes!"

"Yes, Nnarami Obawani was here at the Embassy two days ago, but he left…and was among those reported dead today.

"Are you sure?"

"He was positively identified by the letter 'A' on his arm."

That's what a fraternity brand turned out to be good for.

I started to regress. I began doing things that I had done during Rami's and my glory days, those two weeks before I headed for Success. I tied my hair up in that old purple bandana, ran over the backs of my tennis shoes, treated my stretch marks with cocoa butter, bought Slim-Fast and Lean Cuisines, and got the "My Man Is An Alpha" keychain back from Kern, who, bitch though she was, was very understanding. (Tony wasn't, though. "Your man is *not* an Alpha," he said.) Luke went to a local TV station and got me a copy of a Howard University feature program that Rami had appeared on.

I felt frustrated and useless! On the day that he and I had met in the library, I was writing a paper for a mortuary science class at UDC. Rami and I talked about funeral service at length, including my insistence on being the one to take care of my family and friends. I had explained to him that caring for the deceased is one of the most intimate acts I know, and that I was not comfortable placing that trust in anyone other than myself for those who are close to me. But Rami was somewhere, close to me and dead, and there I was, able to do absolutely nothing for him. I prayed every day that someone had handled him professionally and with care.

Every day I scanned the newspaper for accounts of the civil war in Somalia, but those events remained overshadowed by America's struggles in the Persian Gulf. Finally, though, about four days after Derrick's call, there was a short article with a photo of Rami in the morning edition of The Washington Post where I read the account of what was believed to have happened to him. It was as Derrick had reported, but with more detail.

Later that same day I picked up a paper that was laying around at the funeral home (to check the day's death notices)…and immediately thought I had gone berserk! There was the article about Rami again, but on this reading, I knew about things that were not in the article, and new information appeared that hadn't been there before! I knew the names of all the people who were supposed to be in the house, even though they weren't mentioned. And I learned that Rami's father could not be reached for comment at press time because he, an Ambassador to Singapore, was away on business.

I didn't tell anyone that I thought I was slowly losing it. I kind of liked the idea of going crazy; it seemed like the right thing to do! Besides, I could not wrap my mind around the idea that Rami was gone for good. I saw him in my dreams every night, and could hear him speak to me when I *knew* I was awake: *"I'm here,"* he said.

I was wracked with guilt. Surely people would find it pompous and vain of me to think that I could have prevented Rami's death, so I couldn't bring myself to talk about it...except with A.J.

"What do you think? Do you think if I had stayed here instead of going to South Carolina, things would have turned out differently, and this summer he would have been here with me instead?" Whew! I was reaching!

A.J. sighed. "I was hoping you wouldn't feel that way, Joe. Yes, I do think everything might have turned out differently. That's why I feel so *guilty*—because I told him not to press you about going to South Carolina. I'm sorry."

A.J. was a master of psychology. With somebody else to comfort, I didn't feel as bad!

"That's okay. I probably would have gone anyway. And so would he."

"You think?"

"Yeah, I think," I reassured A.J./myself.

Over those next couple of weeks (especially with school starting again) Baltimore got more and more inconvenient, so staying at Tony's place accomplished two tasks for me: one had to do with my physical proximity to work and school, and the other was all in my head. Being back with Tony allowed me to say that my *ex*-boyfriend had died, rather than my *ex-ex*-boyfriend. By moving back in with Tony, I effectively restored Rami's status as my boyfriend only *once* removed.

A memorial service at Howard was scheduled for early September. I called Derrick to let him know, but he wasn't going to be able to attend.

"How're you holding up, Joe?"

"Well, it's been a couple of weeks now, but I'm still feeling a little crazy."

"Me, too. I really feel sorry for Christina. She and his mom cleaned out his apartment early this week."

"Christina?"

"That's his girl."

Derrick had given Assette a name. And my title. And my sympathy. Had he smiled at her? Hugged her? Asked him to "straighten Rami out" for her, too? (No, of course she wouldn't do anything like that.) Shit.

"Oh! I'm sorry, Joe. If it's any consolation—"

"No-no! Don't worry about it. You sure you won't come?"

"Pretty sure. It's okay, though. I've made my peace with what happened. God gave Rami and me plenty of opportunities to spend quality time this summer before he left, and we really made the most of it."

"That's great," I said flatly, still smarting from the name thing. Then I started thinking about every opportunity I had foolishly, *deliberately,* wasted with Rami.

"You be there for both of us. Say a prayer for me, and call to let me know how it went."

"Sure."

"I love you, Joe."

"You, too, Derrick."

Nnarami's memorial service was nice, but uneventful. I can certainly appreciate any ritual designed to celebrate a life and assuage the pain of loss, but…I think a funeral with a viewing of the body is by far the most valuable, so not having one there could best be described as nice, but not very memorable. I'm sure many of us still did not believe what had happened, but seeing *something* would have helped to confirm that the death had really happened. Reportedly, Nnarami's body had been buried immediately, according to Somali custom (hence, no need for a morgue).

Anyway, several bro's spoke thoughtfully and eloquently. I listened intently, with a dual purpose in mind: to learn something more about who Rami was, and to stay focused so that I wouldn't have time to look around and recognize Assette! I was glad nobody made a fuss over her, Rami's "widow." I also decided that I was glad, after all and somewhat, not to be in her position. My pain could not have been as acute as hers.

I was so busy trying not to see Assette that I thought I missed seeing someone I thought I knew. I believed I had caught a glimpse of the Marine Corps chaplain that I worked with often during military funerals at Maxwell's, but by the time I made my way over to where he was, he was gone.

I had my own "burial" afterwards. I went through all of my things, gathering mementos to place in a small wooden box: the slip of paper he'd first written his number on, the strap from his gym bag, the notes on the Alpha stationery, a piece of the gift wrap from my tennis shoes, my hair bows, the ticket stubs from a movie we went to, the calendar where I'd crossed off the days I was away from him in South Carolina, the newspaper articles, a couple of photographs he definitely was not posing for, and the gold-wrapped box still containing his black and cream bowtie.

Ironically, lots of changes had taken place and I was busier than ever at Maxwell's. Jackie Anderson left to open her own funeral home. Darian went on maternity leave, her assistant, Donald, had quit to go to work at the city morgue, and Pat's husband had been fired. In short, most of the young people and all the eligible embalmers were gone, so all of the work fell to me.

I didn't mind at all; I loved embalming. The problem was that Maxwell's was one of the larger-volume funeral homes in DC, and being in the Southeast quadrant of the city (notorious for crime), few of the cases were ever simple or easy.

In order to embalm, dress, casket, cosmetize, and do hair for 10 to 12 cases per week, I was at work almost all day long. I missed most of my mortuary classes because I could not get away. I would arrive at 9:00 am and work steadily until 5:00 pm. If there were no first viewings or wakes, I had the option of going to class or going home for something to eat and to relax for a while, but invariably I'd be right back at the funeral home late that evening. Most nights, I didn't leave until after 2:00 am. Stepping out into a street in Southeast any time from dusk 'til dawn is highly likely to get a person caught up in a random hail of bullets.

I asked Tony either to come with me and help so that I could leave earlier, or at least to meet me there when I was ready to come home so that I'd have an escort. He indicated that he didn't believe I was really working that late, and refused to do either. I called A.J., who was deathly afraid of funeral homes. But he came and sat at my desk in the office, a stone's throw away from the prep room, and we talked (or sometimes not) over the roar of the embalming machine while I worked:

"So tell me again…*why* isn't *your man* here with you?"

CHAPTER 41

Darian returned from maternity leave just in time for me to take a vacation, so I drove to Gary to spend another Christmas break. Kenji went with me, strapped into the front seat of the car. I thought it was cute. My mother was shocked!

"You know what that's all about, don't you?" she asked.

"What? Who, Kenji?"

"It's got a name?"

"A wardrobe and a godfather, too!" I bragged.

"Oh, Lord. Poor thing," she said, sadly. "Don't you know? That's one of the things people do when they've had an abortion."

Tony and I rang in the New Year together, but from then on, it was as if he had launched a campaign of terror against me! We argued for a solid week, building each day on something I had done or said to quit the previous day's bickering. We got so far away from what we were fighting about...basically, he didn't have any ground to stand on in the original argument, so he kept picking on me about new things, to try to confound and confuse me, diffuse the situation and place the blame on me.

At the end of that terrible week, Tony just figured he would put his hands on me, and a fistfight ensued. I knew I was not a very convincing liar, so I was not about to be battered and then go around looking stupid, making lame excuses for poorly covered-up bruises on my body. Nope!

Ray pulled me off of him. I called Irene, whose boyfriend lived near the apartment, and told her I was leaving! and could her guy come over to help me get my stuff out? She called B-head and asked him to come over and check on me. Meanwhile, she called Sheila and they borrowed a car and drove out to PG County. When they all arrived, I let them into the apartment and we started hauling my boxes out of the living room (I hadn't unpacked from my move from the house), taking turns so that someone was always down at the cars keeping watch. On one of my trips back inside, Tony called me into his room.

"You don't have to leave," he said.

"Yeah, I gotta go. This isn't working out."

"We can work it out, but not if you leave."

"How do you figure we can work it out?"

"Lynn, I been trying to change, but you make it hard. I just don't understand you sometimes."

"I'm not hard to understand. I'm just trying to be happy."

"I can make you happy, but you gotta stay. You know I'm the only man for you. Come on."

"Well, they've already loaded up a lot of my stuff."

"I'll help you unload it."

I went into the living room, where Irene and Sheila were on their way out the door with a trunk and two boxes.

"Hold up, y'all. I just talked with Tony, and he said I don't have to leave."

Irene: "What?! Have you lost your damn mind?"

Sheila: "Joe, it's 2:00 in the motherfuckin' morning, and we just woke somebody up to borrow their car to drive all the way out here from Silver Spring because you called talkin' 'bout you wanted out!"

Irene: "We moving your shit!"

Sheila: "Naw, fuck it! Let her stay her stupid ass here if she wants to! But I tell you what…you and Tony gotta move that shit back in here your own damn selves!"

Tony walked into the living room while they were bombing me out.

"I don't know what the fuck he did to you, or why you think you ain't nothing without that no-good—"

208

"Whoa, whoa, whoa! You don't talk about me in my own house!" Tony said to Sheila.

Little bitty Sheila walked over and stood toe-to-toe with Tony. "I'll talk about anybody I want, anywhere I want to, you punk-ass motherfucker!"

"Bitch—!"

Ray emerged from his room. "Look, y'all gon' have to break this up, and I'mmo have to ask you to leave."

Irene and Sheila left the apartment, slamming the door on their way out. Ray went back into his room. I waited for Tony to put on some clothes, and then we went outside to retrieve my things from the car.

Irene, Sheila, and B-head were standing on the sidewalk in a little group, arms folded. They turned their backs to us when we approached them, but pointed in the direction of the car.

On our second trip back into the apartment, we found Ray standing in the living room, looking out the window at the parking lot.

"What you doin', man? You gon' help?" Tony asked.

"Just watch this."

Tony and I looked at each other quizzically. What was he talking about? We put our load of things in Tony's room and left the apartment again. Ray was no longer in the living room.

When we got outside, Sheila, Irene, and B-head were standing in the same place…with their hands up! Ray was pointing a gun at them!

"Ray, what are you doing?!" I yelled. He smiled smugly and didn't say anything.

"Ray, man, cut that out," Tony said, but Ray just continued to smile.

"This is against the law! It's kidnapping!" Irene yelled.

"You're no cop!" Sheila protested. We had often joked about Ray, who at 35 years old was desperate to be a cop, except nobody seemed to want him on their police force. But Ray had changed jobs since I met him. He was indeed a police officer...of some sort...in some county.

"I'm sorry. Yes, he *is* a cop, *now*" I told them.

"Then where's your badge? Show us your badge!" Irene demanded.

Three police cars came screaming up the side street and stopped, some on the street, and some in the parking lot. Police crawled out of the bushes on the side of the building and from the parked cruisers, all with their weapons drawn.

"What in the hell did you do, Ray?" I asked.

Ray still didn't talk until another officer approached him. Then he put his gun away and showed him some form of identification, while other cops frisked my friends. Ray told him he thought someone was going to get hurt during the "confrontation." The police found a small stick under B-head's jacket, and reprimanded him. Then they talked to me, and reprimanded me for letting people into the apartment where I was not a tenant. Ray shook hands with them all, then retired back to the apartment. Tony and I retrieved the last of my things, as B-head left and Irene and Sheila stormed off, vowing to have nothing else to do with me.

The next evening, Ray told me that the management had requested my immediate departure. I moved to a place I couldn't afford in a complex just down the street, and a "remorseful" Tony came with me.

CHAPTER 42

We moved on February first, vowing to make a fresh start. I really meant it, but *somebody* obviously had his fingers crossed behind his back. During the first two weeks, Tony usually arrived at home no earlier than 2:00 am. He would have some cockamamie story about being out working on his car, even though he was the type of guy who couldn't tell an alternator from his asshole (and I hope most of you missed that double entendre). In the interest of keeping the peace and making a fresh start, I didn't argue with him.

As I mentioned, it was February again, and time for what was becoming my annual mid-winter ritual. (I guess you can tell how I liked to ring in a new year!) The stick turned blue. I did, too.

"I ain't seen no pads or nothing around in a long time. What—you pregnant or something?" Tony smiled in a smug kind of way.

"Pretty much."

Unlike the first pregnancy when I knew without a doubt what had to be done, I was conflicted about this baby, and it had nothing to do with the baby at all. I would feel good about the future if Tony came home at a reasonable time, so the next day at work I'd stay upstairs in the chapel away from the prep room fumes, and wouldn't drink anything other than water. After one of Tony's late nights "working on his car," I'd be so pissed off that I would drink coffee and caffeinated soda and embalm without a mask on! After the fourth or fifth such caffeine morning, I drove past Maxwell's into Northwest, DC and straight to the "Medical Professional Building," forgetting that you can't get the procedure done on the spot. Instead, the receptionist offered to schedule an appointment for me, and although I could guess it would be soon, I didn't know when I'd be as angry again.

Tony brought home another teddy bear. I was thrilled and named it Kirby before I did the math:

$$Kenji = 1^{st} \text{ aborted baby}$$

$$vs.$$

$$Kirby = 2^{nd} \text{ baby}$$

All things being equal, what was missing?

"aborted" = Abort it!

I pictured Kirby sitting snugly between Kenji's outstretched arms and legs in their matching T-shirts, and thought about how cool it was to have these replacements for my babies. Now, I'm a sucker for a good metaphor, but I snapped out of it the very next minute when another image flitted across my mind—the agonizing scraping business that would earn me that second bear, that would make it right for Kirby to be there.

Then the realization that Tony wasn't confused or conflicted at all, that he was simply and clearly showing me what I should do *pissed me off.* True, I was highly suggestible, but I was not a stupid-ass, and I was not about to take advice from one!

My mother came to visit Bill and his wife that month. They'd just had a baby and were packing up to move from Baltimore into a new house closer to DC. I drove to Baltimore to see her, and we went out for some dinner. I ate like a pig, then ordered dessert.

"You weren't hungry, were you?" Lorraine joked.

"Famished!"

"Better watch out, or you'll be getting fat."

"Well, I'll take that as my cue…"

"Your cue for what?"

"I have something to tell you."

"Oh, no you don't!"

"Maaaa!"

"You're pregnant!"

"Pretty much."

Lorraine looked down, put her hands up to her head, shook it, then let out a deep sigh. "What are you going to do?"

"I'm keeping this one. I can't do that thing again, ma."

"I know, I know." She looked up at me across the table, taking me in from the chest up.

I wasn't even two months pregnant, but already I felt out of control of my body. It was a feeling that every inch of my uncombed hair and mismatched sweats reflected.

"Well, you don't have to be a slouch just because you're pregnant. We'll go get you some clothes tomorrow."

"Thanks, ma."

"Hmmm…I wonder what your grandmother Nettie is going to say. *You* tell her!"

CHAPTER 43

I finished serving my year-long apprenticeship at Maxwell's on April 1st and happily handed in my resignation. Boy, was I glad to get my baby away from those fumes!

Tony had agreed to take care of all the bills and everything while I wasn't working so that I could relax, finish my classes and exams, and prepare for graduation from mortuary school. Then the phone bill arrived. Because I was sitting around with nothing to do most of the day, and having friends and family far and wide, it was horrendous! Then my student loan payment was due, my car needed a couple of repairs, and I needed more maternity clothes. Instead of admitting that he could not afford to keep me, Tony bitched and penny-pinched, and penny-pinched and bitched some more.

Besides that, there were the cards, balloons, candy and gifts that he kept bringing home.

"Everybody's just happy for me because I'm having a baby," he explained as I read a poem called "Baby-Maker" from some woman at the post office, and munched on the Tootsie Rolls from the bank teller's gift he brought home a few days before.

"*You're* not having a baby. *I* am. And I don't know these women, so they couldn't possibly be so happy for me."

By the end of April, I felt better to be living out of my car and sleeping on Darian's loveseat.

My U.D.C. graduation exercises were held the first weekend in May. Tony did not attend. My mother, my brothers, and A.J. were there, though. Even Sheila and Irene came, having grudgingly forgiven me for my part in their kidnapping at the hands of Ray. The biggest surprise, though, was that my favorite sands, Derrick, had flown in from California! He gave me flowers and asked me to come and visit him after the baby was born.

Communication with Tony had broken down to almost nothing. We could not talk about anything without arguing: money for the baby (he didn't want me to file for child support), the baby's religion (even though he hadn't attended a church service before or since that Easter he followed me there), the correct time…it didn't matter. And he tried one last time to squirm out of child support by suggesting we skip down to the courthouse and get married. Or that we move back in together.

My money was running out, so I got a job waitressing from 3:00-11:00 pm at an Italian restaurant, where it was fun for the clients to suggest names for the baby and to make bets about its sex. My bosses, the three brothers who owned the place, were real cool. They made sure I took frequent breaks to put my feet up and eat, and just generally looked out for my well-being.

"Make sure Antonio gets you some vegetables today, *hai capito?*"

"If there's nobody back in the bar, you go and get off your feet."

"Don't pick that up. Have one of the guys do it."

The only times they got upset with me was when I would hide all the ashtrays in my section and growl at the customers; they could see I was pregnant, and yet they still insisted on smoking, some of them. They were trying to kill my baby!

During slow periods, they did not mind my friends dropping by to visit (without ordering anything), but the Vittaro brothers got really bent out of shape the few times that Tony stopped in.

"That's his car? The new Corvette? And you're driving—sorry!—that piece of shit?"

"Why are you working, in your condition?"

"You don't live with him? Then why isn't he here every day to see you?"

"If I EVER see him do anything out of line…I'll kick his ass!"

Yeah, my bosses were real cool!

Everything was so cool at my job, and I was such a happy girl that I didn't squawk about working on my birthday.

Irene and A.J. came to see me at Vittaro's to wish me a happy birthday. The brothers let me take an extended break, so we kicked back in the bar room at a corner table. At some point, though, the conversation became reminiscent of the one I'd had with my parents two years before…

"You know, I just have to say this," Irene began. "I don't know if you agree with me, A.J., but look at you, Joe—"

The baby hormones were growing my hair down my back, my nails were long and strong, my breasts had swollen to a C-cup, and my legs were plump. For a pregnant woman, I had it going on! I had a neat job with cool bosses, I was eating well…yes, look at me!

I grinned. *Heehee!*

"—what the *fuck* are you so happy about?"

I blinked, then blinked again and shook my head. Like my mother's left hook, I truly didn't see that one coming! A.J. put his hands up as if to shield himself either from any culpability from Irene's comment or from my reaction to it. My armpits started aching.

"What do you mean?" I asked her.

216

"I mean, you're *unmarried* and *pregnant* by a man—excuse me, a *boy*—who's always cheating on you and doesn't want to help take care of you or your baby, you're going to the *free clinic*—"

"I *like* the free clinic! I wouldn't want to be sitting around waiting for some snooty private doctor all day."

"—you're *homeless,* you're a *waitress*, you're about to be on *welfare*, you're not finished with *school*—"

"I'm outta school!" Eeuuw. I sounded like Miss Bowie High.

"No, you're not," A.J. interjected. "She means Howard, not UDC. Don't get me wrong, though. I mean, there's nothing *wrong* with UDC..."

"Have you thought about it, Joe? You're a mess, your life's a mess! What do you have to offer that baby?" Irene challenged.

"It won't be like this for long!"

"Okay, so that means you have a plan, right?"

"Yeah!"

"Then let's hear it."

"Well..."

There was silence as they waited for me to come up with a plan for my life. I hadn't thought beyond August 1st, when Darian's husband would return from his tour of duty in the Army and I would indeed be out on the street. I'd worn out my welcomes with both Bill and Luke, and Hattie had said no to my living with her with a baby. The baby was due in late September. I'd have to stop working for a while. But after I passed my licensing exam in November, I'd have my full funeral director's license!

"I'll be fully licensed in November, and I'll go back to work."

"Didn't you just leave funeral service?"

"Only for a while, because I'm pregnant."

"Okay, then. You're talking about November. The baby will be almost 2 months old and you *think* you'll be ready to go back to work at a funeral home. It's May, Joe. MAY. Get us from tomorrow through November," Irene challenged.

Silence. *I like the free clinic?*

"Uhhhh…"

Silence. *I'm outta school?*

"Ummmm…"

Silence. *Cheating, no support, waitressing, welfare, homeless, no education, now through November…*

"All right, no. I can't. Shit."

We all shifted condiments around on the table. "Damn! Well, what in the HELL am I supposed to do?" I whined as suddenly, I saw my situation from A.J. and Irene's point of view. It was right at that moment that I awoke from the deep walking sleep I had been in all my life, and joined the land of the living. I became self-aware. I began, finally, to think.

A.J. lifted his head. "I've got an idea. If you go back to Howard and change your major to something you have the most credits in—English, I think, right?—then you probably only have a few classes left to finish."

"Riiiight! I've taken all of my electives already, so all I have left are major courses, whatever I choose."

"So you think you might go back and finish school?" Irene asked.

"It's not a bad idea, especially if I really have only a few classes left."

A.J. pulled some Howard catalogues out of his briefcase. "I can tell you for sure in a second," he said, thumbing through one of them.

"Eight classes!" was his verdict. "That's four per semester. Piece of cake!"

"Eight classes? Eight classes! Is THAT all? I've been holding myself back for lack of only eight classes?"

"Something like that."

"Well, then, yes! I'm going back to school!"

"Why are you going back to school?" Irene asked, being really thick!

"I don't know! What? To finish?" I guessed. Irene frowned, so I continued. "No. But yes! To finish, so that I can have a degree and some options."

"But Joe, how are you going to get from here to there?"

A.J. jumped in again. "Basically, Joe, what Irene is asking you to do is map it out for yourself and decide how you're going to make it happen. So what is it you have to do?"

They were making me tired.

"I have to get in school?" I said.

"Yeah, that's easy. Just fill out the application."

"I have to find a place to live," I added.

"Being in school will take care of that. Apply for housing. Don't mention the baby."

"Then I have to have the baby."

"You'll have health insurance once you're back in school, so you can have the baby at Howard Hospital."

"Really? Yeah! That's right! No more free clinic?

"No more free clinic."

"And no D.C. General, where they treat you like trash and won't give you your sonogram picture because you don't have any money?"

"They did *what*?" A.J. asked, concerned.

"Never mind. Hey, this is fun!" I was really getting into all the planning and strategizing. Things were falling neatly and easily into place—school, housing, medical insurance—I guess because I was finally doing the right thing. *That's what happens when things fit.* By comparison, if you're involved in things you're not supposed to be, everything's an uphill struggle, like trying to force square pegs into round holes.

Both A.J. and Irene shook their heads, smiling at me.

"What next?" I asked, excitedly.

"Child care," Irene suggested.

"I don't know of anybody who'll watch a newborn, so I'll take some time off at first—I would want to do that, anyway—but after that, it's off to class it goes!"

"You're going to take the baby to class?" A.J. asked.

"I don't see where I really have a choice."

"Maybe. You can probably stagger your course load so it's like, two classes in the fall while the baby is still little, and then six in the spring. But let's wait to cross that bridge when we come to it," A.J. said. "Same goes for what you'll do after you finish school. At any rate, you'll have more options than you have now."

CHAPTER 44

Suddenly, my pocket calendar filled with appointments and deadlines and things to do. I was busy every day from early in the morning until time for work.

After the time it took to reapply and be readmitted to Howard, I had only a couple of weeks to find housing suitable for the baby and me. There was an unobtrusive building on the edge of campus—I had passed it many times before and never noticed it—for Howard faculty, staff, retirees, graduate students, and families. My mother sent me the money I needed for first month's rent and security deposit. Darian's husband didn't mind putting up with me for 2 more weeks until the apartment was ready for me to move in.

Darian gave me her son's crib. My grandmother sent me her credit card and I bought a very inexpensive bedroom set. I found a rocker, dining table and chairs at the thrift store. All the other little household items I got cheaply from K-Mart. Once I put it all together, it was a neat little one room that belonged to me.

I surveyed my humble little home, the first place I ever lived on my own, and got sad thinking that I would again be sharing it in about a month's time—for good. And already I had decorated to suit someone else's taste (I hoped the baby liked Winnie-the-Pooh).

As I sat on my bed and contemplated the crib and its decorations, a BIG BUG ran across the floor underneath it:

tiptiptiptiptiptiptiptiptiptiptip!

Barely any furniture in the apartment, and hardly a scrap of food...why was this bug *picking* on me? And even though the windows were closed, it sounded like the ambulances and police cars were right there in the apartment! I wondered how the baby would ever sleep. I cried.

CHAPTER 45

School began the next week with the usual "Back-to-School" meet and greet. I stopped to say hello to my sorors, a mix of old and new ones, then tried to go on my merry way. They didn't need me hanging around. I felt like I was bad for Sigma Image: unmarried, pregnant, old and still in school. My sorors wouldn't hear of it, though, and pulled up a chair for me to get off my feet.

There was little traffic at our booth, as usual. Then a lovely young lady with a thick New York accent stopped by. Once she noticed me sitting there, she turned her attention away from our information table and seemed totally taken with my burgeoning belly. I wanted the sun to melt me into the sidewalk. I could just imagine her walking over to the next booth or joining her friends and going, "Did you see that trifling, old pregnant Sigma they got over there?"

After she moved on, I told my baffled sorors "Told you so" (but of course they didn't know what I was thinking), and went home. I couldn't be sure that she would form a negative opinion about Sigma just because of me. But I did know that she would be ill equipped to form any opinion at all because she walked away without asking one question, and without taking any information—because of me.

I actually enjoyed my classes. Before, they had been a real drag, stuff that I had to take if I wanted to go to medical school. But English—woo hoo! And German—viel spass (that's German for "that joint was a lot of fun")! I was having a great time in school!

A month into the semester, the baby came, and she took all day to do it. I woke up to get ready for my 8:00 am Shakespeare class, but cramps and diarrhea prompted me to call my mother.

"I'm really sick, but I can't take any medicine!"

"What's wrong?" she gasped.

"I had diarrhea as soon as I woke up, and now my stomach hurts."

"You're not sick, silly!" she laughed at me. "That's the baby coming! Go to the hospital. Hang on, I'll be on the next flight out!"

I made a couple of calls to my family, A.J., and the English Department, and then one for a cab to drive me about a minute down Georgia Avenue to Howard University Hospital. I wished I had walked; it woulda made for a cool story to tell the baby at some later time when she wanted to borrow my car or something. The cabbie charged me a whopping $5.00, so I made him get me a wheelchair and wheel me inside to Admissions, too. I found myself already checked in and was wondering how when I caught a glimpse of A.J. as a nurse wheeled me up to my room, where I settled in for the day's activities.

Word of my imminent motherhood spread throughout campus and my circle of friends, and it seemed like everyone I knew dropped by the hospital during the day on various lunch breaks or what-not to wish me good luck. I was especially glad to see A.J. when he walked into the room, especially since I didn't have a chance to thank him for getting me checked in earlier. He had a happy grin for me, too…that is, until he did a double take and I considered the view he was taking in. I had *felt* covered up because I couldn't see underneath the sheet that was tenting my spread-apart knees. On the other side—the doctor's side—my stuff was completely exposed, with all kinds of tubes snaking out of it.

A.J. stopped dead in his tracks in the doorway, and both of our faces dropped.

"Hey, ummm…how ya doing?"
"Uh, fine."
"Well, uh, okay."
"Okay, uh, see ya."
"Yeah, bye."

Mom and my grandmother made it in around 3:00 pm, and everyone else returned after work: Luke, his new girlfriend, and her son; Bill, his wife, and my nephew; Irene, Sheila, A.J., Darian, her husband, and their son. So my daughter, Samantha Lynnette ("little Lynn"!), had a genuine birthday party when she was born at 7:30 pm on—did I mention this coincidence?—A.J.'s birthday, September 27th.

Grandma stayed at Bill's and helped with my nephew, and mom stayed in my one room with Samantha and me. Two weeks later I had lost all my maternity weight, and decided to go back to class. Mom was due to leave another two weeks after that, so I took the baby to a few classes with me, to get used to it. As it turned out, she didn't have to tag along very much; A.J. finagled his work schedule so he'd be completing some contract work that his computer company did for Howard's School of Business, and would be able to sneak over to the apartment to babysit. Mom and grandma went back to Gary after a month.

CHAPTER 46

At the beginning of November I began studying seriously for my funeral director's license exam with two other apprentice funeral directors that I knew from mortuary school. They came to my apartment after work three days a week. Most of those days, A.J. was there making us dinner or entertaining Samantha while we studied. My study mates watched him with incredulity.

Since they were in funeral service, they knew Tony and the whole sordid story, and were happy I was no longer with him. Still, we'd begin most of our study sessions with industry gossip, especially about Tony.

"I am so glad you left that boy alone. Do me a favor—don't ever go back!"

"I saw him at the Medical Examiner's Office the other day, and I had a little talk with him, yeah, girl. I said, 'You ain't no kind of man, not even showing up when your baby is being born.'"

"But I didn't tell him," I clarified.

"Still. He shoulda been checking on you, and when he couldn't find you all day, he shoulda took his sorry ass over to the hospital looking for you."

Just then, A.J. called to say he was on his way over.

"Oh, good, because the baby just started crying. I'll see you in a minute."

"Tell me something," my friend continued as I hung up the phone. "That fine thing that's always over here? Now that's a real man! Why aren't you with *him*?"

All I could do was shake my head. "I used to like him like that," I laughed, "when I first met him. But he wasn't interested. He didn't want me."

Did he tell you that?

Didn't he? No, but he just played me off until I stopped looking like I had a mad crush on him.

"Well, I don't know about all that, but we don't want to see you go back to that other asshole. You seeing anybody else?"

"Oh, no!" Who would I "see"? I hadn't even thought about it.

The suggestion came from Darian's husband, who, of course, was privy to all of my business through Darian. I didn't mind; you gotta know that when you tell one married person something, you've told both of them. Anyway, he asked, "Do you have *any* male friends that you haven't slept with?" I didn't know how to take that at first, but I decided that he hadn't meant to be condescending. (But, wow! Was *that* what my problem was?)

Well, as a matter of fact…aha! There was Derrick, my favorite sands! (…and Rami's friend, and Irene's ex-lover, but I had to admit…) I was attracted to him.

The next day, I was downstairs waiting for AJ to arrive at the apartment building, and it struck me that he, too, was a male friend I had never slept with. I asked God for a sign.

"Lord, if he's the one for me, please give me a sign. Show me…*something.*"

A.J. rounded the corner and began walking up the walkway to the front steps where I was sitting. I stretched my neck forward, wrinkled my brow, and looked straight at him—then to the left of him and to the right of him, and then up at the sky—*hard.*

He stopped walking and looked all around himself, too. "What?!" he asked, nervously.

"Oh, nothing. Come on."

Mom visited again. She gave me $300 and told me to get myself a microwave.

"Where are you getting all this little extra money?" I asked her. My mother had retired early, which was why she had so much free time and energy to spend in DC, but I couldn't account for all the extra money she'd given me: that summer at "Success", the new car, the deposit on the apartment, and then for the microwave.

"Well, I promised I wouldn't tell you, but A.J.'s been giving it to me to give to you. Everything except the car."

"Wow. Why didn't he just give it to me himself?"

"He didn't think you'd accept it from him."

"Why not?"

"Well, you *can* be stubborn. And proud."

"Yeah, I guess you're right!" I grabbed the Sunday sales papers off the kitchen table and flopped down on the bed to begin pricing microwaves. My mother seemed to be waiting for some more conversation to take place. She didn't move, but stood right where she was, just watching me.

"So that's it." she said, flatly.

"Huh?"

"That's *it*? You don't have anything else to say? No more questions?"

"Aaahhh…no?"

"Don't you want to know WHY he's been giving you the money?"

"Because I needed it?"

"You *gotta* know, Lynn."

My armpits… "Know what?"

"You couldn't be *that* blind. A.J. is in *love*…with *you*!"

"How do you know that?"

"We talk. And it's plain to see! Do you love him?"

"I guess so, but not like that."

"Well, *ever* like that?"

"Maybe, sure, when we first met. But it took too long for him to respond. He wasn't interested, so I left it alone."

"But he responded?

"I think he was waiting for me to stop acting like a lovesick puppy-dog. Then he remembered my *name*, and we got to be *friends*. That's all."

"Ah-ha! I see."

"See what?"

"You both fell in love, just at two different times. So instead of getting together and having a hormonal whirlwind love affair, you ended up with a really beautiful friendship where you trust each other and love each other deeply. What you have is like a marriage. Married people aren't groping each other all day long, but they know they're in love. You and A.J. have been so easy and comfortable that you haven't even noticed!"

"That's nice, but I want some romance!"

"What has A.J. done that's *not* romantic?"

"I guess, but still…I like the idea of the hormonal whirlwind!"

My mother looked exasperated. I was being really thick.

"That's why you're in the predicament you're in now!"

I blinked and my jaw dropped open. I couldn't believe she went there!

"I'm sorry. I shouldn't have said that. Listen, you can have your whirlwind, Lynn. All you gotta do is decide that that's what you want, and stop being stubborn! I think you're *still* attracted to A.J. You're keeping him around just like you've been hanging on to Kevin McDonald since you were a toddler. And God *knows* A.J. is attracted to you, even through all…this!

"You can't, or rather, you *shouldn't*, try to build a relationship around sex, darlin'. Don't get me wrong—it's a *good* thing—but sooner or later you've got to get up and *do* something, be productive, *together*. Problem is, most couples can't get past the sex and all the bullshit that comes with it in order to get to that. Luckily, you and A.J. already have the good stuff down, and whenever you decide, you can have the rest."

"Well, what about the day I asked for a sign to let me know, and there was nothing?"

"You asked for a sign?"

"Yeah."

"From God?"

"Um-hmm."

"For what?"

"To tell me if I'm supposed to be with A.J."

"And what happened?"

"Nothing."

"But you asked for a sign."

"*Yes.*" Now my mother was being really thick!

"You ever hear the joke about the man clinging to his roof in the middle of a flood?"

"No."

"Three different people floated by and tried to help him, but he said, 'No. God is going to save me.' Well, he drowned, and when he went to Heaven he asked God why He didn't save him. God said, 'Stupid! I sent three boats!'"

A.J. stopped by for a visit later that evening. As he talked with my mother and played with Samantha, I watched him and replayed scenes from our relationship, intending to look for those three rowboats...except I started at the beginning, and found it exceedingly difficult to get past his initial three-time rejection of me:

FIRST MEETING:

"Hel-*lo*. I don't think I've had the pleasure of making your acquaintance yet. My name's A.J. Who are *you*?"

"I'm Lynn. Pleased to meet you."

"The pleasure's all mine. Do you eat here often?"

"No, I'm not on the meal plan," I laughed. "I'm just here with my roommate."

"Well tell your roommate to be sure to bring you back, all right? Promise me you'll come back."

"I promise."

"Good. And save me a seat next to you."

SECOND MEETING:
"Hey, A.J.! Over here! Hi! Look—I saved a seat for you."

"Have we met before?"

"Umm, yeah, a couple of days ago when I came with my roommate and you said next time to save you a seat."

THIRD MEETING:
"Hi, A.J.! It's good to see you."

I-know-I-know-you-from-somewhere. "Uh, what's your name again?"

"Lynn."

Okay, so it was one meeting and only two rejections. Still, I had thought that there was something there, but obviously I was mistaken. I felt silly and foolish. I was embarrassed. I was pissed off.

Never again, I told myself.

He usually called a cab when he was ready to go, but this time A.J. asked me to drive. He definitely was not himself on the ride home. He looked nervous, and he sat in the backseat as if he were a passenger in a taxi.

I tried to chatter mindlessly during the several-block drive to A.J.'s house, but I found out he had his own agenda when he cut me off mid-ramble.

"What did I do wrong?" he asked.

"What in the *world* are you talking about?"

"Why don't you want to be with me?"

"What are you *talking* about?"

"Stop it, Lynn. You *know* what I'm talking about."

Never again. "No, really. Honest, I don't."

"I've been chasing after you since we first met, freshman year."

"Oh, you want to be funny…"

"Do I look like I'm trying to be funny?"

I glanced in the rearview mirror at him. He had his serious face on, but…*Never again.*

"Well, what do you mean, you've been chasing after me since we first met? Since we first met *which time*, seeing as I had to meet you three different times before you ever remembered who I was!"

"Now what are *you* talking about?"

"I'm talking about how stupid I felt when every time I saw you, I had to remind you who I was. We met at least three times!"

"Well, yeah, okay. But don't tell me you were pissed about *that*…"

"Hell yeah, I was pissed about it—I still am, now that I stop to think about it! That made me feel *really* insignificant, so I just said, 'Forget it!' I figured you weren't interested, so I went on about my business—"

"I *was* interested—"

"Well you sure had a funny way of showing it, uh…uh…whatever your name is!" I spat.

"—but it's just that I didn't recognize you—"

"That's exactly what I'm saying!"

"—because you kept changing your hair!"

?

"My *hair*?"

"Yes, your *hair*," A.J. replied curtly. "And you kept that up all freshman year. One day it would be wild and curly, the next day it would be hanging straight down, then it would be in a ponytail, then you colored it, then you cut it all off…"

"You're right! I did change it all the time, didn't I?"

"You haven't stopped, either. You just slowed down. Now it's more like, two styles a year."

"I guess it woulda been hard to recognize me."

"Yes, and it was a little embarrassing. I was telling all my friends about this woman I met, describing you to them, then the next time I saw you, you'd be almost totally different. And I didn't want to *admit* that I didn't know who you were."

"Well, I wish you hadda. I've been holding a grudge against you all this time!"

"Why?"

"I just figured you didn't like me, so when I stopped acting like I wanted to be with you, that's when you started hanging out with me."

"I finally got used to you changing, that's all."

"Damn."

"Damn."

"So."

"So."

"What?"

"What?"

"Here we go…" I announced as I pulled up in front of his house. "That'll be six dollars and fifty cents."

A.J. didn't move.

"Here's your hat, what's your hurry?" I giggled.

"I'm in love with you, you know," he said, quietly.

Well, there. He had finally said it.

My armpits…were calm. A.J.'s words sounded surprisingly natural. It was as natural as the way—for five

233

years—he had shown me he loved me, hugged me, respected me, told me I was smart and pretty and special and cool, made me feel protected, celebrated my victories, consoled my disappointments, advised and encouraged me, taken me on dates, spoiled me, broken my heart just a little, investigated boyfriends, and loved and respected women.

"Here we go…" I repeated.

"Huh?" A.J.'s eyes in the rearview mirror looked stricken. He must have thought I was ignoring him, or worse yet, rejecting him!

It was just…what was I going to do with somebody who seemed perfect for *me* when I didn't even know who *me* was, what *I* was all about? Maybe I should have said that. Maybe I should have just told him I didn't know *what* to say. I was hoping at least to come up with a good song or line from a movie or something.

Meanwhile, A.J. got out of my car, walked up his stairs and into his house. I didn't think about the fact that he could have been walking out of my life right then. All I knew was that I had known real love…and that I wasn't ready for it yet. So I just sat and watched him leave as I cried quietly somewhere on the inside.

But only for a minute. I had things to do.

ORDER FORM

The Era of My Youthful Ways

NAME: _____

ADDRESS: _____

_____

PHONE: _____

E-MAIL: _____

check or money order

a. Number of copies: _____ x $14.95 = _____

b. DC Residents add 5.75% sales tax: _____
   ($0.86 per book for DC Residents)

c. Shipping & Handling*: _____

d. TOTAL: _____

*S&H:
1-3 books: $4.95; 4-6 books: $9.95; 7-10 books: $14.95; 11-20 books $25.95

DETACH AND MAIL THIS ORDER FORM TO:
Croness Publishing; P.O. Box 1869; Washington, DC 20013

ORDER FORM

The Era of My Youthful Ways

NAME: _____

ADDRESS: _____

_____

PHONE: _____

E-MAIL: _____

check or money order

a. Number of copies: _____ x $14.95 = _____

b. DC Residents add 5.75% sales tax: _____
   ($0.86 per book for DC Residents)

c. Shipping & Handling*: _____

d. TOTAL: _____

*S&H:
1-3 books: $4.95; *4-6* books: $9.95; *7-10* books: $14.95; *11-20* books $25.95

DETACH AND MAIL THIS ORDER FORM TO:
Croness Publishing; P.O. Box 1869; Washington, DC 20013